"That kiss had nothing to do with technique."

"No—it was about power! About winning. Because you can't bear to lose. Especially to a woman."

Judd took a long, shuddering breath. "Maybe it was about feelings."

She wasn't going to go there, not with Judd, so she said, "Maybe it was about ownership."

But the bitterness in his voice had shocked Lise. If she weren't pregnant by him, might she have softened, asked him what he meant by "feelings"? But all her intuition screamed that if Judd knew she was pregnant, he would insist on marrying her—because it was his child she was carrying.

His. Ownership indeed.

Sandra Field

EXPECTING HIS BABY

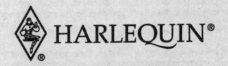

TORONTO • NEW YORK • LONDON
AMSTERDAM • PARIS • SYDNEY • HAMBURG
STOCKHOLM • ATHENS • TOKYO • MILAN • MADRID
PRAGUE • WARSAW • BUDAPEST • AUCKLAND

ISBN 0-373-12257-8

EXPECTING HIS BABY

First North American Publication 2002.

This edition published by arrangement with Harlequin Books S.A.

® and TM are trademarks of the publisher. Trademarks indicated with ® are registered in the United States Patent and Trademark Office, the Canadian Trade Marks Office and in other countries.

Visit us at www.eHarlequin.com

Printed in U.S.A.

CHAPTER ONE

THERE was a woman in the bed.

An astonishingly beautiful woman.

Judd Harwood stood still, gazing at the sleeping figure under the white hospital bedspread. He must have the wrong room. It was a man he was looking for, not a woman. Yet instead of leaving and asking someone for better directions, Judd stayed exactly where he was, his slate-gray eyes focused on the bed's occupant. Her right shoulder and upper arm were swathed in an ice pack. Her face was very pale; the livid bruise marring the sweet curve of her jawline stood out in sharp contrast to the creamy skin. Had she been in a car accident, or fallen on the ice encrusting the city streets? Or had it been something worse? Surely she hadn't been assaulted.

His fists curled at his sides in impotent anger. Could it have been her husband? Her lover? He'd flatten the bastard if he ever got his hands on him. Flatten him and ask questions afterward. And how was that for a crazy reaction? A woman he'd never even met, knew nothing about.

He wasn't into protecting strange women. He had better things to do with his time.

His jaw a hard line, Judd continued his scrutiny. The woman's brows were delicate as wings, her cheekbones softly hollowed; he found himself longing to stroke the silken slope from the corner of her eye to the corner of her mouth. An infinitely kissable mouth, he thought, his own mouth dry. Her eyes were closed; he found himself intensely curious to know what color they were. Gray as storm clouds? The rich brown of wet earth? Her hair was

5

red, although that word in no way did justice to a tumble of curls vivid as flame.

Flame...

Blanking from his mind a surge of nightmare images, Judd gave himself a shake. He didn't have the time for this; he needed to find the fireman who'd saved Emmy. Thank him as best he could and then go back to his daughter's bedside. Emmy was sedated, the doctor had assured him of that, and wouldn't wake for hours. But Judd wasn't taking any chances.

So why was he still standing here?

Scowling, purposely not looking for the woman's name on the chart at the foot of the bed, Judd strode out of the room. A nurse was hurrying toward him, her flowered uniform a splash of color in the bare corridor. He said, "Excuse me—I'm looking for the fireman who was admitted earlier this evening...he rescued my daughter and I need to thank him. But I don't even know his name."

The nurse gave him an harassed smile. "Actually it was a woman," she said. "I don't believe—"

"A *woman?*" Judd repeated blankly.

"That's right." Her smile was a shade less friendly. "They do have women on the fire and rescue squads, you know. Room 214. Although I don't believe she's recovered consciousness yet."

Room 214 was the room he'd already been in. The room with the woman lying so still on the bed. Trying to regain some semblance of his normal self-control, Judd said abruptly, "I shouldn't have made the assumption it was a man. Thanks for your help."

"If you need to talk to her, tomorrow would be better. She won't be released before midmorning."

"Okay—thanks again."

The nurse disappeared into a room across the hall. Slowly Judd walked back into Room 214. The woman was lying exactly as she had been a few moments ago, the smooth line of the sheet rising and falling gently with her breathing. He walked closer to the bed, staring at her as though he could imprint every aspect of her appearance in his mind, teased by a strange sense that she resembled someone he knew. But who? He couldn't put a finger on it, and he prided himself on his memory. Surely he'd never seen her before; he could scarcely have forgotten her. The purity of her bone structure. The gentle jut of her wrist bones. Her long, capable fingers, curled defencelessly on the woven coverlet.

Ringless fingers. Did that mean she didn't have a husband?

Her fingernails were dirty. Well, of course they were. She was a firefighter, wasn't she?

This was the woman who'd saved his daughter's life; Judd didn't even have to close his eyes to remember the horrific scene that had greeted him when the cab from Montreal's Dorval airport had dropped him off in the driveway of his house.

Clutching his briefcase, Judd saw three fire trucks parked on the lawn, their red lights flashing into the darkness. Yellow-jacketed firefighters shouted back and forth, barking orders into two-way radios. Water hissed from coiled gray hoses. Great billows of black smoke, rising from the roof, were licked by flames that appeared and disappeared with the wicked unpredictability of vipers. For a moment Judd was stunned, his feet rooted to the ground, his heart thudding in heavy strokes that overrode all the other sounds. He'd known fear before. Of course he had. Some of the situations he persisted in subjecting himself to saw to that. But he'd never known anything as devastating as the terror that clamped itself to every nerve and muscle in his body when he pictured Emmy trapped in that heat, in the choking smoke and vicious destruction of fire.

A tall metal ladder was angled against the wall of the house, reaching toward the windows of the family wing. The wing where Emmy slept...

Judd ran forward, yelling her name. Four policemen jumped him, grabbing his arms as they fought to restrain him. A fifth went flying when Judd flung him aside. And then Judd saw a small bundled figure thrust through the window into the waiting arms of the firefighter on the ladder. He gave a hoarse shout, and as the fireman passed the bundle to another man waiting further down the ladder, the policemen finally released him.

He ran across the frozen, snow-patched lawn faster than he'd ever run in his life. As the fireman transferred Emmy to his arms, the panic in her eyes cut him like a knife, the small weight of her catching at his heartstrings.

Holding her with fierce protectiveness, he climbed into the back of the waiting ambulance. But as he did so, Judd threw a quick glance over his shoulder, in time to catch part of the roof collapsing in a shower of sparks that under any other circumstances might have been eerily beautiful. A blackened beam struck the firefighter who'd shoved Emmy through the window. The helmeted figure staggered and almost fell, and in dreadful fascination Judd watched the fireman at the top of the ladder seize a yellow sleeve, hauling the other firefighter's body over the charred sill by sheer, brute force. A cheer went up from the watchers on the ground. Then Judd turned away, shielding Emmy from the leaping flames and surreal, flickering lights...

Judd came back to the present with a jolt, licking his lips. Emmy had been pronounced out of danger from the smoke she'd inhaled. Because of her sedative-induced sleep, he'd taken this opportunity to find the firefighter to whom he owed a debt of gratitude that could never be repaid.

The woman on the bed.

She couldn't be much over five-seven or five-eight. Her features lacked the perfection of Angeline's: her nose slightly crooked, her mouth a touch too generous. Angeline was his ex-wife, mother of Emmy. An internationally known model, who wouldn't have been caught dead with dirty fingernails.

He didn't want to think about Angeline, her poise and stunning looks, her seductive body and cool, midnight-blue eyes. Not now. He'd divorced her four years ago, and had seen almost nothing of her since then.

The woman on the bed stirred a little, muttering something under her breath. Her lashes flickered. But then her breath sighed in her chest and she settled again. Somehow, in the midst of a maelstrom of smoke and flame and the night's darkness, this woman had found Emmy and carried her to the ladder, into the waiting arms of the other firefighter. To safety.

Judd walked to the foot of the bed, frowning slightly as he started reading the neatly typed words on the chart. Then the woman's name leaped out at him. Lise Charbonneau. Age twenty-eight.

His frown deepened, his eyes intent in a way some of his business associates would have recognized. Angeline still went by her own name, which was also Charbonneau. And Angeline's young cousin had been called Lise. He'd met her at the wedding, all those years ago.

It couldn't be the same person. That would be stretching coincidence too far.

But Lise at the age of thirteen or so had had flaming, unruly red hair, and cheekbones that even then gave promise of an elegance to come. She'd also had braces on her teeth and the gawkiness of a foal new to the field, and no social graces whatsoever. Her eyes, though, had been as green as spring grass, almond-shaped eyes that were already beautiful.

He searched his memory. Hadn't she been living with Angeline and Marthe, Angeline's mother, because her own parents had died tragically? And hadn't they died in a house fire?

Was that why Lise Charbonneau had become a firefighter?

Angeline's cousin responsible for saving Angeline's daughter…what a strange and unbelievable irony. Speaking of which, he'd better try to reach Angeline. He himself was always fodder for journalists; he didn't want Angeline hearing about Emmy's escape on the late-night television news.

But then the woman in the bed shifted again, moaning slightly under her breath. He stiffened to attention, going over to stand by the bed, watching her struggle toward consciousness. And to pain by the look of it, he thought grimly, reaching for the buzzer that was pinned to the pillow by her head, and with an effort restraining himself from taking a strand of her vivid hair between his fingers. Hair that could warm a man's heart. He said gently, "It's okay, I'm calling the nurse."

Her eyes flickered open, closed again, then opened more widely, focusing on him with difficulty. They were a clear, brilliant green, exquisitely shaped. Tension rippling along his nerves, Judd waited for her to speak.

The man's outline was blurred, throbbing in tandem with the throbbing in her shoulder. Lise blinked, trying to clear her vision of a haze of pain and sedatives, and this time he was more distinct. More distinct and instantly recognizable.

Judd. Judd Harwood. Standing beside her bed, gazing

at her with an intensity that made her heart lurch in her breast. He'd come for her, she thought dizzily. Finally. Her knight in shining armor, her gallant prince... How many times, as a teenager, had she fantasized just such an awakening? His big body, so broad-shouldered and narrow-hipped, his square jaw and fierce vitality: she'd known them—so she'd thought—as well as she'd known her own body. Known them and longed for them. Hopelessly. Because all those years ago Judd had been in love with Angeline.

But now it was as though all her adolescent dreams had coalesced, and she'd woken to find the first man she'd ever fallen for watching her in a way that curled heat through every limb. She'd been madly and inarticulately in love with him back then, no matter that he was married to her cousin. How could she not have loved him? To a lonely and impressionable teenager, his looks and personality had had the impact of an ax blade, splintering her innocence. Since then, of course, she'd been hugely disillusioned, all her trite little daydreams shattered on the hard rocks of adult reality.

Judd Harwood. Unfaithful husband of her beloved cousin Angeline. The man who had refused Angeline custody of her own daughter, who'd been too busy amassing his fortune to be anything other than an absentee husband and father. The jet-setter with a woman in every major city in the world.

But what, she wondered frantically, fighting to overcome the fuzziness of her thoughts, was he doing standing by her bed? And where was she anyway? Because this was no dream. The dull, thudding pain in her shoulder and the sharp needles of agony behind her eyes were all too real. So was he, of course. His thick black hair now had threads of gray over the ears, she noticed in confusion. But his eyes were still that chameleon shade between blue and gray, and his jawline was as arrogant as ever.

"Where—" she croaked.

"I've called the nurse," he said in the deep baritone that she now realized she'd never forgotten. "Just lie still, she'll be here in a minute."

"But what are you—"

The door swung open and on soft rubber heels a nurse came in the room. She went straight to the bed, smiling at Lise. "So you're awake—good. And not feeling so great by the look of you. I'll give you another shot, that'll help the pain in your shoulder." With calm efficiency, she checked Lise's pulse and temperature, asked a few questions and gave her the requisite painkiller. "It'll take a few moments to take effect," she said briskly, and glanced up at Judd. "Perhaps you could stay until she's asleep again?"

"Certainly," Judd said.

With a last smile at Lise, the nurse left the room. Judd said evenly, "You're the Lise I met years ago, aren't you? Angeline's cousin? Do you remember me? Judd Harwood."

Oh, yes, she remembered him. Lise said, "I don't want to talk to you."

She'd planned for this to come out crisply and decisively, edged with all the contempt she harbored for him. But her tongue felt like a sponge in her mouth, and her words were scarcely audible even to herself. In huge frustration, she tried again, struggling to marshal her thoughts in a brain stuffed with cotton wool. "I have nothing to say to you," she whispered, then let exhaustion flatten her to the pillow.

"Lise..." Judd bent closer, so close she could see the cleanly sculpted curve of his mouth and the small dent in his chin. A wave of panic washed over her. She turned her head away, squeezing her eyes shut. "Go away," she mumbled.

He said tightly, "I'll come back tomorrow morning. But I want you to know how grateful—oh hell, what kind of a word is that? You saved my daughter's life, Lise, at the risk of your own. I'll never be able to thank you enough."

Her eyes flew open. She gaped up at him, trying to take in what he was saying, remembering the nightmare search from room to room, the dash up the attic stairs and the child huddled at bay in the corner. "You mean the fire was at *your* house?" she gasped. He nodded. In growing agitation she said, "All I heard was that the owner was away and there was a baby-sitter and a little girl. No names."

"My daughter. Emmy."

"Angeline's daughter—she's Angeline's just as much as yours!"

"Angeline left when Emmy was three," Judd said in a hard voice.

"You refused her custody."

"She didn't want it."

"That's not what she told me."

"Look," Judd said flatly, "this is no time for an autopsy on my divorce. You saved Emmy's life. You showed enormous courage." Briefly he rested his hand over hers. "Thank you. That's all I wanted to say."

His fingers were warm, with a latent strength that seemed to race through Lise's body as flame could race along an exposed wire. "Do you really think I need your gratitude?" she cried, hating his nearness, despising herself for being so achingly aware of it. She was damned if she was going to respond to him like the lovesick adolescent she'd been; she was twenty-eight years old, she'd been around. And he was nothing to her. Nothing. She tried to pull her hand away from his, felt agony lance from her elbow to her shoulder, and gave an inarticulate yelp of pain.

Judd said tautly, "For God's sake, lie still. You're acting as though you hate me."

With faint surprise that he could be so obtuse, she said, "Why wouldn't I hate you?"

To her infinite relief, he straightened, his hand falling to his side. An emotion she couldn't possibly have defined flickered across his face. In a neutral voice he said, "You grew up with Angeline."

"I adored her," Lise announced defiantly. "She was everything I always wanted to be, and she was kind to me at a time when I badly needed it." Kind in a rather distant, amused fashion, and kind only when it didn't inconvenience Angeline; as an adult, Lise had come to see these distinctions. Nevertheless, during a period in her life when she'd been horribly lonely, her cousin had taken the trouble to teach her how to dance, and given her advice on her complexion and how to talk to boys. Had paid attention to her. Which was more than Marthe, Angeline's mother, had done.

"Adoration isn't the most clear-eyed of emotions," Judd said.

"What would you know about emotions?"

"Just what do you mean by that?"

"Figure it out, Judd," Lise said wearily. The drugs were starting to take effect, the throbbing in her shoulder lessening; her eyes felt heavy, her body full of lassitude, and all she wanted was for him to go away. Then the door swung smoothly on its hinges again, and with a flood of relief she saw Dave's familiar face.

Dave McDowell was her co-worker, almost always on the same shifts as she. She liked him enormously for his calmness under pressure, and for his rock-solid dependability. He was still wearing the navy-blue coveralls that went under their outer gear; he looked worn-out. She said warmly, "Dave...good thing you were on that ladder."

"Yeah," he said. "You were really pushing it, Lise."

"The little girl wasn't in her room. For some reason she'd slept in the attic. So it took me a while to find her."

Judd made a small sound in his throat. Emmy slept in the attic when she was lonely, she'd told him that once. And he'd been away for four days. So if she'd died in the fire because she couldn't be found, the blame could have been laid squarely on his own shoulders.

Unable to face his own thoughts, Judd turned to Dave. "My name's Judd Harwood—it's my daughter Lise rescued. If you were the man on the ladder—then I owe you a debt of thanks, too."

"Dave McDowell," Dave said with a friendly grin that lit up his brown eyes. "We make a good team, Lise and I. Except she doesn't always go by the manual."

"Rules are made to be bent," Lise muttered.

"One of these days, you'll bend them too often," Dave said with a touch of grimness.

"Dave, I weigh less than the guys and I can go places they can't. And I got her out, didn't I?"

"You scare the tar out of me sometimes, that's all."

Lise said a very pithy word under her breath. Dave raised his eyebrows and produced a rather battered bouquet of flowers from behind his back. "Picked these up on the way over. Although you'll be going home tomorrow, they say."

"Come and get me?" Lise asked.

"Sure will."

"Good," she said contentedly.

"Might even clean up your apartment for you."

Lise said with considerable dignity, "A messy room is the sign of a creative mind."

"It's the sign of someone who'd rather read mystery novels than do housework."

"Makes total sense to me." Lise grinned.

Judd shifted his position. The easy camaraderie between the two of them made him obscurely angry in a way he couldn't analyse. So Dave was familiar with Lise's apartment. Was he her lover as well as her cohort at work? And what if he was? Why should that matter to him, Judd? Other than being the woman who'd saved Emmy's life, Lise Charbonneau was nothing to him.

Yet she was beautiful in a way Angeline could never be. A beauty that was much more than skin deep, that was rooted not only in courage but in emotion. He said brusquely, "I'll be staying in the hospital overnight with my daughter. I'll drop by in the morning, Lise, to see how you are."

"Please don't," she said sharply. "You've thanked me. There's nothing more to say."

As Dave raised his brows again, Judd said implacably, "Then I'll be in touch with you later on. McDowell, thanks again—your team did a great job."

"No sweat, man."

Judd marched out of the room and down the corridor toward the elevator. He wasn't used to being given the brush-off. Hey, who was he kidding? He was never given the brush-off. Women seemed to find his looks, coupled with his money, a potent combination, so much so that he was the one used to handing out brush-offs. Politely. Diplomatically. But the message was almost always the same. Hands off.

Lise Charbonneau hated his guts. No doubt about that. Dammit, she'd been scarcely conscious and she'd found the energy to let him know she thought he was the lowest of the low. And all because of Angeline. Who in the end had dumped him as unceremoniously as if he'd been a pair of boots she was tired of wearing. Trouble is, at the time that had hurt. Hurt rather more than he was prepared to admit. During the eleven years it had lasted, he'd done his level best to hold his marriage together, and to preserve the intensity of emotion that had poleaxed him when he'd first met Angeline. But he'd failed on both counts. Hence his propensity for brush-offs whenever a woman showed any signs of getting too close, or having any ambitions toward matrimony.

Been there. Done that.

He'd have to phone Angeline first thing in the morning: assuming that she was home in the elegant chateau on the Loire that was the principal residence of her second husband, Henri. Who was, incidentally, no longer richer than Judd. Judd, however, couldn't lay claim to a string of counts and dukes in his ancestry. Far from it. If he rarely thought about Angeline, he even more rarely recalled his upbringing on the sordid tenements of Manhattan's lower east side.

The elevator seemed to take forever to arrive, but finally he was pushing open the door to Emmy's room. The little girl was lying peacefully asleep, just as he'd left her. She had her mother's dark blue eyes and heart-shaped face; but her long, straight hair was as black as his, and she'd inherited both his quickness of mind and ability to keep her own counsel. He'd loved her from the moment she'd been born. But only rarely did he know exactly what she was thinking.

As he reached over and smoothed her hair back from her face, she didn't even stir. He'd wanted to make the same gesture with Lise, although from very different motives. Motives nowhere near as pure as the love of a father for his daughter.

He hadn't seen the last of Lise. He knew that in his bones. Although if she were involved with Dave, he'd be one heck of a lot smarter to keep his distance. If he hadn't liked the first brush-off, why would he like the second any better? And he'd never tried forcing himself between a woman and her lover. Never had to, and he wasn't about to start now.

Put Lise Charbonneau out of your mind, he told himself, and focus on getting some sleep. Tomorrow he had to look after Emmy, insurance agents, the police and contractors for repairs. He didn't need the distraction of a flame-haired woman who thought he was the scum of the earth. Scowling, Judd lay down on the cot that the nurses had provided and stared up at the ceiling. But it was a long time before he fell asleep, because two images kept circling in his brain.

Emmy sleeping in the attic because she was lonely.

And the dirt under Lise's fingernails. Dirt from a fire in which she'd risked her life for Emmy's sake.

CHAPTER TWO

THREE days after the fire and her shoulder was still killing her, Lise thought irritably. She hated being off work and having so much time to think. And even more she hated feeling so helpless and ineffective. It was nearly noon, and all she'd accomplished so far today was to have a shower, make her bed and buy a few groceries. The cabbie had been kind enough to carry them upstairs to her apartment door. But she'd had to put them away, one thing at a time, because she could only use her left arm. She wasn't sleeping well, she'd watched far too much TV the last three days, she'd read until her eyes ached, and yes, she was in a foul mood.

She pulled a chair over to the counter, climbed up and reached for the package of rice. But as she lifted it in her good hand, she bumped her sore shoulder on the edge of the cupboard door. Pain lanced the whole length of her arm. With a sharp cry, she dropped the rice. It hit a can of tomatoes, the bag split and rice showered over the counter and the floor.

Lise knew a great many swearwords, working as she did with a team of men. But not one of them seemed even remotely adequate. Tears of frustration flooding her eyes, she leaned her forehead against the cupboard door. What was wrong with her? Why did she suddenly feel like crying her eyes out?

She needed a change. That was one reason. Desperately and immediately, she needed to alter her lifestyle.

It wasn't the first time she'd had this thought. But its intensity was new. New and frightening, because if she

19

quit her job at the fire station, what else would she do? She'd worked there for nearly ten years. She didn't have a university degree, she had not one speck of artistic talent, and anything to do with the world of commerce reduced her to a blithering idiot. She couldn't even balance her checkbook, for Pete's sake.

So how could she quit her job?

With her good hand, she reached for the box of tissues on the counter; but as she tugged one free, more rice pellets rattled to the counter. The counter needed wiping. The sink was full of dirty dishes. Her whole life was a mess, Lise thought, blowing her nose and clambering down from the chair. And how she loathed self-pitying women. Maybe she'd make herself a large cherry milk shake and eat six brownies in a row. That might give her the energy to clean up the rice. If not the refrigerator.

Somewhat cheered by the thought of the brownies—she'd made them from a packaged mix, with considerable difficulty, yesterday—Lise pulled the pan out from on top of the bread bin. But as she opened the drawer for a knife, someone knocked on her door.

It was a very decisive knock. Puzzled, she walked to the door and peered through the peephole.

Judd Harwood was standing on the other side of the door.

The last person in the world she wanted visiting her.

She yanked the door open, said furiously, "No, I do not want to see you and how did you get past security?"

"Waited until someone else opened the main door," he said mildly. "You look god-awful, Lise."

"Make my day."

"Looks like someone ought to, and it might as well be me."

"Oh, I don't think so."

But as she tried to push the door shut, he neatly inserted

his foot in the gap and pried it further open. She seethed, "Judd, I'll holler blue murder if you don't go away."

He gave her a charming smile, although his eyes, she noticed, were cool and watchful. "I've got a favor to ask you," he said. "It concerns Emmy, not me, and it's important. Won't you at least hear me out?"

"Do you always use other people to gain your own ends?"

In a voice like steel, he said, "I happen to be telling the truth. Or is that a commodity you don't recognize?"

"In you, no."

"If we're going to have a no-holds-barred, drag-'em-out fight, let's at least do it in the privacy of your apartment," he said, and pushed past her to stand in the hallway.

He was six inches taller than she, and probably seventy pounds heavier. Not to mention his muscles. Lise slammed the door shut and leaned back against it. "So what's the favor and make it fast."

He stepped closer. "You've been crying."

Between gritted teeth she said, "The favor, Judd."

"What's wrong?"

"Nothing. Everything. I can't go back to work for a whole week, my right arm's useless and I'm going nuts. Do you know what I did all day yesterday? Watched reruns of *Star Wars*—for the third time. And what else would you like to know? What are you doing here anyway—slumming?"

"I told you—I have a favor to ask you."

"I've read about you. In *Fortune* and *Time* magazine. About all your fancy houses, your cars and planes, your women. The international airlines you own. All of which are euphemisms for power. Power and money. And you expect me to believe that *I* can be of use to you? Don't make me laugh."

In sudden amusement Judd said, "You don't have red

hair for nothing, do you? I didn't have time for coffee this morning—how about I put on a pot and we sit down like two civilized human beings and have a reasonable conversation.''

"I don't feel even remotely reasonable when I'm anywhere in your vicinity," Lise snapped, then instantly wished the words unsaid.

"Don't you? Now that's interesting," Judd said silkily.

She couldn't back away from him: her shoulder blades were pressed into the door as it was. "Judd, let's get something straight. I don't like you. I don't like what you did to Angeline. So there's no room for small talk between you and me. Tell me what the favor is, I'll decide if I want to do it and then you can leave."

"I'll leave when I'm ready."

She tossed her head. "Macho stuff. I get a dose of that at work, I don't need it at home."

"Are you ever at a loss for words?"

"I can't afford to be—I work with men," she retorted. As, unexpectedly, he began to laugh, his sheer vitality seemed to shrink the hallway; she caught her breath between her teeth, wishing she'd gone out for coffee this morning and was anywhere but here. But Judd would have tracked her down sooner or later: that much she knew. Realizing she was conceding defeat, swearing it would be only temporary, she said grudgingly, "Caffeinated or decaf?"

"Doesn't matter. Where's the kitchen?"

She winced. "The living room's through there. I'll only be a minute."

"Got a man hidden behind the stove, Lise?"

The gleam of humor in his slate-gray eyes was irresistible, and suddenly she heard herself laughing. Laughing as if she liked him, she thought in panic. "Behind my stove is not a place any self-respecting man would want to go," she said, adding, "Watch where you step," as she led the way into the narrow galley kitchen.

Judd stopped in the doorway. "Well," he said, looking around. "If Dave cleaned up your apartment the other day, he's a better firefighter than a Molly Maid."

"Dave doesn't live here!"

"Is he your lover?"

"What gives you the right to ask a personal question like that?"

He hesitated perceptibly. "I'm not sure. *Are* you and Dave lovers?"

Not for anything was she going to expose the relationship between her and Dave to Judd Harwood's knife-blade gaze. "No comment," she said stonily.

"I see…in that case, I take my coffee black," Judd said. "With honey if you have any. Did you throw the rice at the wall?"

She rolled her eyes. "I was trying to put away the groceries, banged my shoulder on the cupboard and dropped the rice. The bag burst. As you see."

"Rice is a symbol of fertility," Judd said lightly. "Isn't that why they throw it at weddings?"

"Did they throw it at yours?"

His lashes flickered. "No. Angeline was into gold-leaf confetti. Nothing as ordinary as rice." Angeline had never wanted to have a baby; her figure had been more important to her than her husband's longing for children. Emmy's conception had been an accident, plain and simple.

For a moment Lise would have sworn there'd been genuine pain underlying Judd's voice. But the next moment his eyes were guarded, impenetrable as pewter. She'd imagined it. Of course she had. Judd Harwood hurt because of something she'd said? What a joke.

He said casually, "Where do you keep your vacuum

cleaner? I'd better get rid of this mess before you slip on it and break your neck.''

He owned the largest and most luxurious airlines in the world; she couldn't pick up a daily paper and not know that. And he was about to vacuum her kitchen floor? Something so ordinary—to use his own word—had never figured among her romantic fantasies all those years ago. As a teenager, she'd been more apt to picture him maddened by desire, carrying her in his strong arms away from Marthe, from the ugly brick house in Outremont, and the boredom of homework and appointments with the orthodontist.

''The vacuum's in the hall cupboard,'' Lise said edgily. ''I'll wipe all the rice that's on the counters onto the floor.''

''You do that.''

As he left the room, she stared after him. Her whole nervous system was on high alert; any remnants of self-pity had fled the minute Judd had pushed his way into her apartment. But she could handle him. She wasn't an impressionable and innocent teenager anymore; she'd been around the block a few times and learned a thing or two. No, she was more than a match for Judd Harwood. Scowling, Lise fished a cloth from among the dishes piled in the sink and started pushing the rice grains onto the floor. Which could do with a darn good scrubbing.

When Judd came back in, he'd shed his leather bomber jacket and was rolling up the sleeves of a blue cotton shirt. His jeans were faded with wear, fitting his hips snugly. Her gaze skewed away. She said rapidly, ''I still can't use my right arm—I feel such a klutz.''

''No permanent damage, though?'' he asked; she would have sworn his concern was real.

''Nope. Just a Technicolor shoulder,'' she said, and watched his gaze drop.

She was wearing a T-shirt that had shrunk in the drier; it was turquoise with orange hummingbirds flitting across her breasts. The bruise on her jaw was a putrid shade of yellow. How to impress the man of your dreams, Lise thought dryly, and said, "I'll get out of the way while you vacuum. This kitchen's never been big enough for two."

Reaching for the plug, Judd remarked, "Perhaps that's why you haven't married?"

Cordially she responded, "Why couldn't you be faithful to Angeline?"

"I was."

She snorted. "You'll have to do under the cupboards...you wouldn't think one bag of rice could make such a mess."

"Changing the subject, Lise?"

"You're quick," she said with a saucy grin.

"You're so goddamned beautiful," he said with sudden violence.

He couldn't mean it; flattery must be his standard practice when he was anywhere near a woman. Nevertheless, Lise flushed to the roots of her hair. "*Me?* I'm a mess."

"*Thank you, Judd.* That's considered a more appropriate response."

"Maybe in the circles you move in. But I don't want your compliments, Judd. They're as useless as your wedding vows."

He straightened to his full height. "While we were married, I was never unfaithful to Angeline."

"Tell it to someone who cares."

"I could make you care," he said softly.

Her breath caught in her throat. "I don't think so."

"Are you daring me, Lise?"

"No, Judd. I'm telling you I'm out-of-bounds as far as you're concerned. Off-limits. Uninterested."

"We'll see," he said with that same dangerous softness.

"You'd better move—this kitchen, as you so rightly remarked, isn't big enough for the two of us."

Something in his steady gaze caused her to back up. With as much dignity as she could muster, Lise retreated to the bathroom, where she dragged a brush through her tumbled curls and pulled on a loose sweatshirt over her T-shirt. How to stop feeling sorry for yourself, she thought, poking out her tongue at her reflection. Invite a cougar into your apartment. A starving, highly predatory cougar.

Uneasily she gazed in the mirror. Her cheeks were still flushed and her eyes were shining. Stop it, she told herself. He's not a knight in shining armor come to rescue you. His breastplate's tarnished and he abused his vows. Just you remember that.

Unfortunately he was still the most vibrantly masculine man she'd ever laid eyes on. That hadn't changed. Sexy didn't begin to describe him. It went deeper than that to a confidence that was bone-deep, an unconscious aura of power as much a part of him as his thick black hair and deep-set, changeable eyes.

Why did it have to be *his* daughter she'd rescued? She didn't need Judd in her life. He frightened her, she who could force her way through choking smoke and the crackle of flame.

The vacuum cleaner had been turned off. Steeling herself, Lise went back to the kitchen, said politely, "Thank you," and reached for the coffee beans, which were in the container marked Flour. But she couldn't unscrew the lid with one hand.

Judd said, "Here, let me," and took it from her. In utter fascination she watched the play of muscles in his wrist as his lean fingers undid the jar. "Where's the grinder?" he asked.

This was all so domesticated, she thought wildly. As

though they were married. "In the cupboard by the sink. Ignore the muddle."

As he opened the cupboard, two cookie sheets clattered to the floor. "You live as dangerously at home as you do at work," Judd said, and fished out the grinder.

She blurted, "What's the favor, Judd?"

"Coffee first."

With bad grace Lise hauled out the pot, shoved in a filter and located mugs, cream and sugar. "You sure like getting your own way."

"It's how you get to the top—knowing what you want and going after it."

"Judd Harwood's Philosophy of Life?"

Standing very close to her, yet not touching her, Judd said, "You've got a problem with that?"

"What happens to the people you climb over on the way up?"

"You see me as a real monster, don't you?" He grabbed the pot, poured water in it and plugged it in. "The favor's this. Emmy's having nightmares. About the fire. She wakes up screaming that someone in a mask is coming after her. I thought if she could meet you, it might help."

Lise said slowly, "I was wearing an oxygen mask, because of the smoke. And our clothes are very bulky. So I must have looked pretty scary."

"Would you come to the house, Lise?" Judd raked his fingers through his hair. "I know it's asking a lot—using your spare time for something related to work. I just can't stand hearing her scream like that in the middle of the night."

His voice was rough with emotion. And if he was faking that, she was a monkey's uncle. Knowing she had no choice, knowing simultaneously that she was taking a huge risk, far bigger than when she'd blundered her way to the attic, Lise said, "Yes, I'll come."

"You *will?*"

"Did you think I wouldn't?"

"I wondered."

"*I'm* not a monster, Judd. When do you want me to come—today?"

"The sooner the better. She gets home from school around three-thirty."

"Then I'll arrive at four."

"That's astonishingly generous of you."

His smile filled her with a mixture of feelings she couldn't possibly have analyzed. She shifted uncomfortably. "No, it's not. She's a child, Judd, and I know about—well, never mind."

"Your parents died in a fire, didn't they?"

A muscle twitched in her jaw. "I've said I'll come. Don't push your luck."

"I'll send a car for you."

"I'll get a cab."

"Is independence your middle name?"

"I'll take that as a compliment," she said mockingly, and reached up in the cupboard for a couple of mugs. But at the same time Judd stepped closer. Her hand brushed his arm, the contact shivering through her. Then, with one finger, he traced her cheekbone to her hairline, tugging gently on a loose red curl, his every movement etched into her skin. "You're an enigma to me, you know that?" he said huskily.

He was near enough that she could see the small dark flecks in his irises; his closeness seemed to penetrate all her defences, leaving her exposed and vulnerable in a way she hated. She tried to pull back, but somehow his other arm was around her waist, warm and heavy against her hip. Her heart was hammering in her rib cage, a staccato rhythm that further disoriented her. He drew her closer, his gaze pinioning her. Every nerve in her body screamed at her to run. Resting one hand on his chest, Lise tried to push back; but the heat of his body seeped through his cotton shirt, burning her fingers. Heat, the tautness of muscle and bone, and the hard pounding of his heart...she fought for control, for common sense and caution, and all the while was losing herself in the deep pools of his eyes. Then Judd lowered his head and with a thrill of mingled terror and joy Lise knew he was going to kiss her.

She tried once more to extricate herself, pushing back against his encircling arm. ''Judd, don't,'' she gasped. ''Please—don't.''

His answer was to find her mouth with his own, closing off her words with his lips. And at the first touch Lise was lost, for fantasy had fused with reality, and reality was the passionate warmth of a man's mouth sealed to her own, seeking her response, demanding it. Her good arm slid up his chest, her fingers burying themselves in the silky dark hair at his nape. Her body swayed into his, soft and pliant. She parted her lips to the urgency of his tongue, welcoming its invasion; he pulled her against his chest as his kiss deepened. Raw hunger blossomed within her, hunger such as she'd never known before. It did away with constraint, made nonsense of caution. Blind with need, she dug her fingers into his scalp and felt the hardness of his erection against her belly.

The shock rippled through her. She heard him groan her name in between a storm of brief, fierce kisses on her lips, her cheeks, her closed eyelids. As though he were exploring her, she thought dimly, as a mariner would explore the inlets, coves and shores of a newly discovered land. Her breasts were soft to his chest, and the turmoil of desire that pervaded her whole body was like a conflagration. She didn't want to fight it. She wanted to go with it, follow into whatever dangers the flames might lead her.

Break all the rules. As Dave so often accused her of doing.

Like a dash of cold water, the image of Dave's pleasant face thrust itself between her and Judd. She'd sometimes wondered if Dave was falling in love with her; certainly he was her best friend, a man she'd worked with and knew through and through, as only those who work in constant danger can know one another. But Judd...Judd was her enemy. What was she thinking of to kiss him this way, so wantonly? So cheaply?

With a whimper of pure distress, Lise shoved hard against Judd's chest. Like a knife wound, agony ripped its way along her right arm to her shoulder. She cried out with pain, turning her face away from him, involuntary tears filling her eyes.

"Lise—what's the matter?"

"Let go of me," she said raggedly. "Just let go!"

"For God's sake, don't cry," he said hoarsely.

"Judd, let me go!"

As he released her, she sagged against the edge of the counter, her breath sobbing in her throat, and said the first thing that came into her head. "You didn't have to kiss me like that—I'd already agreed to go and see Emmy."

"You think I kissed you as a kind of insurance policy?" he snarled. "Is that what you think?"

"What else am I supposed to think?"

"I kissed you because I wanted to! Because you're utterly beautiful and you've got a temper like a wildcat and you're courageous and generous. Because I craved to taste your mouth and touch your skin. To tangle my fingers in your hair."

Lise's cheeks flared scarlet. Judd was telling the truth, she thought faintly. Every word he'd just said was the simple truth. Or the not so simple truth. "You—you can't do that," she stammered. "You're the man who was married to my cousin. I don't like you, and we live in totally different environments—we're worlds apart in every way that matters. Yes, I'll come and see Emmy this afternoon. But that's it. No more contact. Ever.''

''Do you respond to Dave the way you just responded to me?''

''That's none of your business!''

''Come clean, Lise.''

''It's lust, Judd, between you and me—that's all. Nothing we're going to act on and how do you think I feel kissing a man I despise? Lousy, that's how.''

''You don't even know me!''

''I know Angeline.''

''Impasse,'' Judd said softly.

''So why don't we skip the coffee?'' She ran her fingers through her hair. ''I'm sure not in the mood for small talk.''

''What happened between you and me just then is rarer than you might—''

''Ask the expert,'' she said nastily.

''Don't, Lise,'' he said in a raw voice. ''We don't need to trade cheap shots. Both of us deserve better than that.''

''In your opinion.''

His jaw tightened. ''You're not going to listen to reason, are you? Your mind's made up that I'm the villain of the piece and Angeline—'' he gave a harsh laugh ''—why, Angeline's the blond-haired angel. Grow up, Lise. No marriage breaks up with all the fault on one side. Especially when a child's involved.''

''Why wouldn't you give Angeline custody?'' Lise demanded. ''And don't tell me it's because she didn't want it.''

''What else am I supposed to tell you? It happens to be true.''

She gave an impatient sigh. "And why were you away when the fire started? It was a business trip, wasn't it?"

For once she'd knocked Judd off balance. He stared at her blankly. "You could say so."

She pounced. "You were away with a woman, weren't you? Why else would you be hedging?"

"I was not!"

"You know what I hate about this?" Lise flared. "You're lying to me, Judd. About Angeline. About the women in your life. And yet you expect me to fall into your arms as though none of that matters." Gripping the edge of the counter so hard her knuckles were white, she said, "I wish you'd go. I've had enough of this. More than enough."

"It's not over, Lise," he said with menacing quietness. "Don't kid yourself on that score."

"There's nothing to be over—because there's nothing between us!"

"You're dead wrong. I'll see myself out."

He pivoted and a moment later the door closed behind him. Lise stood very still. Her knees were trembling as though she'd been running uphill for half an hour; her heartbeat sounded very loud in the sudden silence. One kiss, she thought numbly. How could one kiss turn her life upside down?

When Dave kissed her, she never felt anything remotely like the fierce hunger that had enveloped her just now and that had made nonsense of all her rules. Dave's kisses were as pleasant as the man himself. Which might be one reason why she and Dave had never gone to bed together.

She'd go to Judd's house this afternoon, do her best to allay Emmy's fears and then she'd leave. And that would be that. If Emmy was there, Judd could hardly kiss her again.

But if he did, what would she do?

CHAPTER THREE

PROMPTLY at four o'clock the cab turned into Judd's driveway. The ornate iron gates were open, leading into stands of mature birch, oak and evergreens, where the snow lay in soft drifts: a small forest in the midst of the city. Then Lise was dropped off in front of the house. Except it wasn't a house. It was a mansion.

Right out of her league.

The night of the fire she hadn't taken time for anything other than working out where the bedrooms were in the family wing. Now she stood for a few moments, gazing upward. Despite the trampled grass, and the scaffolding against the damaged wing, it was a beautiful house, U-shaped, the lower story built of gray stone, the upper shingled in sage-green cedar. Rhododendrons and azaleas were clustered against the stonework; immaculate snow lay over an expanse of lawn bordered by tall pines. A tree house nestled in the branches of a maple, while a small pond had been cleared for skating. For Emmy, thought Lise, admiring the way the late afternoon sun gleamed orange and gold on the windows.

It was a very welcoming house.

It didn't fit what she knew of Judd Harwood.

She carried her bag of gear across the driveway, climbed the front steps and rang the doorbell. Almost immediately, Judd opened the door. "Please come in," he said formally. "I told Emmy you'd be here soon."

He was wearing dark trousers with a teal-blue sweater. No man should look that good, Lise thought. It simply wasn't fair. His features were too strongly carved to be considered handsome; it was the underlying energy, his sheer masculinity that was so overpowering. She said with a careful lack of warmth, "Hello, Judd, nice to see you," and walked past him into the house.

The foyer with its expanse of oak flooring was painted sunshine-yellow, a graceful spiral staircase drawing her eye upward. An eclectic array of modern paintings intrigued her instantly with their strong colors and sense of design. By the tall windows, the delicate branches of a fig tree overhung clay pots of amaryllis in brilliant bloom.

Color. Warmth. Welcome. The only jarring note was, elusively, the smell of smoke. Confused and disarmed, Lise blurted, "But it's beautiful."

"What were you expecting? Medieval armor and poisoned arrows?"

Patches of red on her cheeks, she looked him full in the eye. "Where's Emmy?"

"In the guest wing—we've had to seal off the family wing. So the playroom's makeshift, and a lot of her favorite toys couldn't be rescued." His mouth tightened. "She was clutching her favorite bear when you found her...she won't let it out of her sight even though it stinks of smoke and I'm sure acts as a constant reminder."

"Plush," Lise said. "She told me his name while I was carrying her out of the attic."

For a moment Judd's eyes were those of a man in torment. "The fire chief figures it was a fault in the wiring. The housekeeper and her husband raised the alarm—they live in a cottage just behind the house, they had family visiting them that night. The baby-sitter had a headache, she'd taken so many painkillers she was out like a light on the couch. If it hadn't been for you, Lise..."

Lise couldn't stand the look on his face; with an actual physical effort, she kept her hands by her side when all she wanted to do was smooth the lines of strain from around his mouth. "If it hadn't been me, it would have been Dave or one of the other firefighters," she said non-committally. "Why don't you take me to the playroom?"

"Yeah…Maryann, the housekeeper, is up there with Emmy." He shoved his hands into his pockets. "What's in the bag?"

"You'll see."

"Here, let me take your coat."

As he reached out for her sheepskin jacket, she quickly slid out of it, not wanting him to touch her. He said, "So you haven't forgotten."

She didn't pretend to misunderstand him. "There'll be no repeat."

"Not here. Not now."

"Nowhere. Ever."

He raised one brow. "Are you daring me, by any chance?"

"Emmy, Judd."

"I didn't get where I am today without taking a risk or two—you might want to remember that."

She said amiably, "Oh, I take risks, too. But I choose my risks. Show some discrimination."

"Whereas I go after every available female?"

"Plus a few that aren't. Me, for instance."

"Lise," Judd said flatly, "are you involved with Dave?"

She could lie, tell him that she and Dave were a number. And if she did, she had the feeling Judd would leave her strictly alone. But she'd never been any good at lying, and she'd waited too long. "There's no easy answer to that question. Yes. No. Neither one cuts it."

"I don't think you are," Judd drawled. "Just as well, considering the way you kissed me."

"And how many women are you involved with, Judd?"

"Platonically, several. But I don't have a lover, if that's what you mean. Haven't had for some time."

His eyes were fastened on her face; he must have been aware of her quickened breathing. "Do you expect me to believe that?"

"Yes," he said in a hard voice, "as a matter of fact, I do."

"Then you're clean out of luck."

"The media can make a hotbed of romance out of a handshake, it's how they earn their keep—you might want to remember that."

She said coolly, "No smoke without a fire."

He had the audacity to laugh. "I shouldn't argue with the expert—but there's no fire without some basic chemistry. Until you came along, I'd been doing just fine without either one."

Into her mind flashed an image she'd never been able to forget: Judd and Angeline in the back garden in Outremont. Locked in each other's arms, kissing in a way that had shattered her adolescent naiveté. "You and Angeline had chemistry."

"Initially, yes."

"So it doesn't last."

"Not if there's too little else to support it."

"Not if one of the partners transfers it elsewhere," she flashed. "Even if I am arguing with the expert."

"You listen to me for a minute! I'm a very rich man—money equals power in our society, and power's an aphrodisiac. So yes, there are women after me. All the time. But, like you, I prefer to exercise choice. And what's easily available isn't always what's desired."

"I'm not playing some sort of hard-to-get game!"

"I never thought you were." Briefly Judd touched her cheek, removing his hand before she could back off. "I

have the feeling you're just being yourself. And you have
no idea how refreshing that is, after the circles I move in.''

"Who else would I be but myself?" she said with some
asperity.

"When we're talking my kind of money, you'd be surprised what hoops people will jump through.'' Restlessly
he moved his shoulders. "Let's go find Emmy—I'll carry
your bag."

She trailed up the stairs behind him, wondering if she'd
ever had such a disturbing or inconclusive conversation.
Had it been a drawing of battle lines? A stating of two
mutually incompatible points of view? Or of Judd's intention to pursue her regardless of her wishes?

Did she want the answer?

The stairs opened into another generous hallway with
an exquisite Persian carpet in faded shades of red and blue.
The two paintings, unless she was mistaken, were a
Matisse and a Modigliani. She should be wearing something by Chanel or Dior, Lise thought with wry humor.
Not khaki pants, a tangerine sweater and loafers, with her
hair pulled back in a ponytail. Then Judd opened a paneled
door. "Emmy?" he called. "Lise is here." And Lise followed him into the room.

It was a charming room, painted eggshell blue, with a
child's four-poster bed canopied in white muslin. Lise's
feet sank into the carpet. "Hello, Emmy," she said.

Emmy was dressed in denim overalls, her straight dark
hair shining in the light. Her blue eyes—Angeline's eyes,
Lise thought with a twist of her heart—were fastened on
the bear in her arms. Plush. Who still reeked of the smoke
of her nightmares. "Hello," Emmy said, and didn't look
up.

Lise hadn't rehearsed any course of action, trusting
she'd know what to do when she got there. She watched
Judd drop her bag on the carpet and walked over to Emmy,

hunkering down beside her. "Your dad says you're having nightmares about the fire."

"Mmm."

Still no eye contact. "I expect I looked very scary," Lise said matter-of-factly. "So I brought my uniform with me, so you can see what it's all for. Why I have to dress up in all that stuff."

Trying not to favor her sore arm too obviously, she pulled out her long waterproof pants with their silver braces, and the boots with the strips of fluorescent tape on them, and began talking about them in a quiet, uninflected voice. She moved to the jacket, the straps for the oxygen tank, and her helmet with its protective shield, trying them all on as she went; and was steadily aware that Emmy was listening, even though the child was giving nothing away. Then, finally, she took out her mask, and saw Emmy's dark lashes flicker. "See, these are the head straps, they're adjustable. And this black coil connects with the oxygen tank I carry on my back. Feel it, you can make it longer and shorter. Sort of like a Slinky toy, did you ever have one of those?"

Tentatively Emmy reached out her hand, poking at the coil. "It changes the way I look," Lise said, and held it up, putting her face behind it. "But it's still me. Nobody scary. Nobody who needs to be in a nightmare." Lowering the mask, she put all the reassurance she possibly could into her smile.

"It's too big for me," Emmy said.

"Yes, it is. It might fit Plush, though."

Emmy blinked. "Do you think he wants to wear it? Isn't he scared of it, too?"

"Why don't we try it on and see?"

With some reluctance, the little girl passed over her bear. Carefully Lise fastened the mask to his face, tightening the straps around his caramel colored fur. "There," she said. "He doesn't seem to mind it, does he? In fact, he looks rather dashing, don't you think?"

"Maryann wants to put Plush in the washing machine with lots of soap so he won't smell of smoke," Emmy said in a rush. "But I don't want her to. I keep him around all the time. That's why he was in the attic with me."

Emmy had given Lise the perfect opportunity to satisfy her curiosity. "Were you in the attic because you were running away from the fire?" she asked with a careful lack of emphasis.

For the first time, Emmy looked right at her. "Oh, no. When my dad's away and I'm lonesome, I sleep in the attic."

And does that happen often?

Fortunately Lise hadn't asked the question: merely thought it. But she was aware of a steady burn of anger that Judd could so cavalierly leave his daughter alone while he went off on business trips. Or so-called business trips, the ones where he was with a woman. How *could* he?

"Well," she said easily, "I'm really glad it was me who found you and Plush. You were both very brave to keep each other company. He's earned a pot or two of honey for that, I'd say—if he's anything like Pooh Bear."

As Emmy gave a small chuckle, Lise's lips curved in response. "A little something at eleven," Emmy said shyly.

To her dismay, Lise wanted very badly to hug Emmy; and knew it would be the wrong move. Too soon. Too much. She said gently, "Would you like to take Plush's mask off?"

Her small fingers very nimble, Emmy loosened the clasps and eased the mask away from the bear. "He likes it better without it," she said.

Lise laughed. "So do I. It has its uses, but it's not what

you'd call comfortable." With no ceremony, she started shoving all her gear back in the bag. "All these clothes make me as fat as Pooh the time he got stuck in Rabbit's front door."

If she'd hoped for another of those sweet smiles from Emmy, Lise was disappointed. The child was clutching Plush to her chest, and in some very real way had retreated from her. Had she, Lise, reached Emmy? Helped in any way that would be lasting?

A tap came at the door, and a plump elderly woman in a flowered housedress came in the door carrying a tray of tea and cookies. Judd introduced Lise to Maryann, the housekeeper, who gave her a disconcertingly keen look before leaving the tray and closing the door behind her. Emmy drank a glass of milk and ate an oatmeal cookie, answering Lise's artless questions with unfailing politeness and no warmth whatsoever. In the course of her job, Lise often visited schools, and rather prided herself on her rapport with children. But whatever her gifts in that direction, they weren't working today, she thought unhappily, wondering why it should matter so much that a small, blue-eyed girl should rebuff her.

It was a relief when Judd got up and said casually, "I'm going to carry Lise's gear downstairs, Emmy, and drive her home. Maryann's in the kitchen and I'll be back in a few minutes. Say goodbye."

"Goodbye," Emmy said, looking at Lise's shoes rather than her face. "Thank you for coming."

"You're welcome," Lise said, infusing her voice with genuine warmth. "It was nice to meet you, Emmy."

Emmy, pointedly, said nothing. Lise trudged downstairs behind Judd. Standing in the gracious foyer, she asked, "Do you think I did any good?"

Judd said ruefully, "I very rarely know what my daughter's thinking, and yes, I would suspect you did. You handled it beautifully, Lise, thanks so much…and now I'll drive you home.''

Lise didn't want Judd within fifty feet of her apartment. Not after the last time. ''I have a couple of errands to run,'' she said, ''I'd rather get a cab. And I'm sure Emmy needs you more than I do. So she won't get lonesome again.''

''Do you think I'm not blaming myself?'' Judd said harshly. ''Give me a break.''

''Angeline always complained about how much you were away.''

His lips tightened. ''I'm sure she did.''

''Is there a phone nearby? For the cab?''

''You're in an almighty rush to be out of here.''

She was; she was terrified he might touch her again, and the alchemy of his body transform her into a woman she scarcely knew. Then Judd took her by the arm, and Lise's whole body tensed. He said tautly, ''I have a proposal…and hear me out before you say anything. Emmy's out of school for the next few days, it's March break. I want to get her away from the house and the smell of smoke and all the repairs, so we're going to Dominica—I have a property there. I want you to come with us.''

''*Me?*'' Lise squawked. ''Are you nuts?''

''I'm both sober and in my right mind,'' Judd said curtly. ''For one thing, I'd like you to be around in case the nightmares persist. Secondly, it's a small way I can thank you for saving her life. And thirdly, you're on sick leave and very obviously at a loose end. I could even add a fourth incentive. It's March in Montreal—wouldn't anyone rather be on a beach in the West Indies?''

Lise had never been south. Never lazed on a tropical beach or swum in a sea the color of turquoise. For a moment sheer longing to do something so irresponsible, so remote from her normal life, caught her in its grip. Palm trees. Papayas and mangoes. A holiday. A real holiday away from emergencies and sirens and the tragedies that inevitably went with the job. Away from weeping women, charred ruins, smashed cars on an icy highway. Away from the three or four men at the station who would never accept her as someone who could do the job as well as they, no matter how hard she tried. She was so tired of it all. Ten years' tired.

A holiday with Judd.

How could she even be contemplating such a move? She was the one who was nuts. Trying to tug free, Lise said in a raw voice, "I can't, it's a ridiculous idea."

"Give me one good reason why you can't go."

For a horrible moment Lise couldn't think of one. "Emmy doesn't want me around," she blurted.

"She'd get over it."

"I'd be using you."

"You let me worry about that."

"Judd, I can't go! I've never in my life gone away with a man who's a stranger and I'm not going to start now."

"Come on, we met years ago, I'm not exactly a stranger."

She stared up at him. He was smiling at her, a smile of such calculated charm that all her alarm bells went off. Judd was obviously expecting her to capitulate. In bed and out? she wondered, and heard herself say, "Anyway, there's Dave."

"There's also the chemistry, Lise. Between you and me. The kind that starts conflagrations."

Willing her knees not to tremble, Lise glared up at him. "Let's have some plain talk here, Judd Harwood. I'll spell it out for you. You're quite a guy. Tall, dark and handsome nowhere near describes you. You're sexy, rich and powerful, your smile's pure dynamite and your body would drive any woman from sixteen to sixty stark-raving mad. Why wouldn't I respond to you? I'd have to be dead in my grave not to. But it doesn't mean a darn thing—I don't even like you, for Pete's sake. So please don't feel flattered that I just about fell into your arms, it's nothing to—''

Judd said flatly, ''Great snow job, and I don't believe a word of it.''

''That's your ego talking!''

''Dammit, Lise,'' he exploded, ''there's something about you that's different. I don't normally ask a woman I've spent less than three hours with to go away with me and my daughter. Especially my daughter. You can trust me on that one.''

''Whether I trust a single word you say is completely irrelevant. I'm not going to Dominica with you. I'm not going to the local grocery store with you. Now will you please call me a cab?''

Judd stood very still, looking down at her. Her eyes were as brilliant as emeralds in sunlight, and her face was passionate with conviction. She wasn't playing hard to get, he knew that in his bones. But she was wrong. Dead wrong.

What *was* Dave to her? And what had Angeline told her over the years?

He couldn't answer either question. All he could do was add two more. When was the last time a woman had said no to him? Or had turned down an all-expenses trip to a tropical paradise?

Never.

He didn't like it one bit. So what was this all about? His bruised ego, as Lise had suggested?

He was damned if this was just a question of hurt pride. It had to be about more than that.

About more than the ache in his groin and his passionate hunger to possess her? His thoughts stopped short. He said tightly, ''I'll call a cab. If Emmy has more nightmares, will you come back?''

"If you're in Dominica, I won't be able to, will I?" Lise said, tossing her head.

The light through the tall windows caught in her hair, an alchemy of gold and copper. His body hardened involuntarily and with an impatient exclamation Judd turned away, taking his cell phone out of his pocket and dialing the nearest cab station. Four minutes, he was promised. So he had four minutes to persuade a stubborn, red-haired woman to change her mind. Casually he turned back to face her. "You're right," he said, "it was a crazy idea, I allowed my concern for Emmy to override my common sense. Sorry about that. Anyway, you must have been south before, lots of times."

"No. How long before the taxi comes?"

"A couple of minutes. Come off it, Lise, you must have been to Bermuda or the Bahamas. Or at least to Florida."

"The furthest south I've been is Boston and who do you think would take me on a romantic tryst to the tropics? The fire chief?"

Why not Dave? "You don't need me telling you you're a beautiful woman. So don't pretend there haven't been men in your life," Judd said tersely.

"Sure there have been. They stick around until the first time I get called out on emergency and I'm gone for six hours. Or until my first string of night shifts when I come home exhausted at 6:00 a.m. and have to sleep all day so I won't be a basket case the next night. Or until they get jealous of me spending all my working hours with men. Be honest, Judd—you wouldn't like it any better than the rest of them."

Her hours of work didn't bother Judd in the slightest; he could put in some pretty horrific hours himself. It was the danger she was exposed to that made the blood run cold in his veins. But he wasn't about to tell her that.

"Dave knows the score," he said, "he works shifts as well. So why haven't you gone south with Dave?"

"He's never asked me," Lise said airily. "Oh, there's the cab. Bye, Judd."

He picked up her bag of gear and followed her outdoors. "We haven't seen the last of each other."

She gave him a dazzling smile as she opened the door of the taxi. "Have a great time in Dominica."

He reached in front of her and deposited the bag on the back seat. When she stooped to follow it, he pulled her into his arms, twisting her around and kissing her hard on the mouth. Before he could lose control, he stepped back, letting his arms fall to his sides. "See you," he said.

Her nostrils flared; her cheeks were bright patches of color. "Over my dead body," she snapped, clambered into the back seat with none of her usual grace and slammed the door. The cab disappeared into the trees round the curve of the driveway.

Ordinarily Judd's next move would be to send an extravagant spray of orchids. Or a bottle of Dom Pérignon along with a big box of the world's most expensive chocolates. Or all three. Somehow he didn't think any of the above would cut much ice with Lise.

So what was he going to do? Let a female firefighter defeat him? Cut his losses and forget he'd ever met her?

He'd seen another side of her upstairs in Emmy's bedroom; allied to a volatile mixture of courage and passion, he could now add sensitivity, warmth and humor. She'd even made Emmy smile. Perhaps, he thought painfully, Emmy needed Lise as much or more than he did.

Need her? He, Judd Harwood, needing a woman? All he needed was Lise's body. He'd better not forget that. If he could only slake his hunger for her, make love to her the night through, he'd be able to put her behind him and forget about her, just as he always had with every other woman but Angeline.

He'd vowed after Angeline left that he'd never fall in love again, and he'd meant every word of it.

The woman wasn't born who could change his mind on that score.

CHAPTER FOUR

LISE leaned her head back on the seat of the taxi. She'd been exaggerating when she'd told Judd she had errands to do. She didn't, not really. She had precisely nothing to do. That was the trouble. She rubbed at her lips with the back of her hand, trying to erase the fierce pressure of his mouth on hers, remembering all too clearly how her heart had leaped in her breast and how every cell in her body had urged her to respond.

Dominica? With Judd? She'd be better off leaping from the top floor of a burning building.

She'd given the cabbie the address of her apartment. So what was she going to do? Go home and scrub the kitchen floor with her one good arm? Watch *Star Wars* for the fourth time?

She could go and see Marthe.

Lise sat up a little straighter. Marthe had been Judd's mother-in-law. Yes, she'd visit Marthe.

It had been many years since a grieving, terrified seven-year-old girl had gone to live with her Tante Marthe and cousin Angeline in the big brick house in Outremont. Not once in those years had Marthe hugged Lise or spontaneously kissed her with warmth and caring; or, for that matter, comforted the nightmares that had racked Lise's sleep after the fire that had killed her parents.

No wonder she'd been unable to refuse Judd's request to try to cure Emmy of her nightmares. What choice had she had?

For as long as Lise could remember, all Marthe's love had been wrapped up in her exquisitely beautiful daughter,

Angeline; finally, when the hurt had threatened to over-
whelm her, Lise had worked out that there was no love
left over for a stray niece. Yet, out of a sense of duty, Lise
still dropped in to visit her aunt, who lived with a succes-
sion of maids and housekeepers in the same ugly mansion
in a French area of the city.

This vibrant mix of cultures, French and English, was
one of the things Lise enjoyed most about Montreal, a city
built on an island in the wide St Lawrence River; in her
leisure time she loved its bistros and brasseries, the live-
liness of its music and its joie de vivre. And it was home
to her now; she'd lived here for twenty-one of her twenty-
eight years.

Half an hour later, having left her gear at her apartment,
Lise was ringing the doorbell of Marthe's house. The maid
led Lise to a formal parlor at the back of the house, where
Marthe was sitting in a pale wash of sunlight writing a
letter. She was wearing a black wool skirt with an impec-
cable blue twinset, as pale a blue as her eyes; her pearls
were perfectly matched, her gray hair rigidly curled.
"Hello, *Tante*," Lise said pleasantly. "Is this a good time
for a visit?"

Marthe offered a powdered cheek to be kissed and os-
tentatiously folded the letter so Lise couldn't read it. "Of
course," she said. "As you know, the hours are long for
me."

Resolutely refusing to feel guilty, Lise said cheerfully,
"Even though it's cold out, the sun is lovely. Are you
writing to Angeline?"

"I haven't heard from her for nearly two weeks,"
Marthe said fretfully, "and I get no satisfaction when I
call the château, she's always out or unavailable. Mind
you, her social life is very important, she mixes with the
very best people, as you know. Last week she was on a
Mediterranean cruise with the Count and Countess of…"

Marthe was launched; Lise settled in to listen and ask the occasional question. Angeline was now in her mid-thirties and did very little modeling, preferring to devote herself to the jet-set crowd. It must be—Lise did a quick calculation—four years since Angeline had spared time on one of her rushed Montreal visits to get in touch with Lise by telephone; there hadn't been the opportunity for a visit. It had been around the period when the custody of Emmy had been settled; she could recall the conversation as clearly as if it were yesterday.

"Emmy will be with Judd," Angeline had said, a break in her beautifully modulated voice.

"Not with you?" Lise asked, appalled.

"Only for the occasional holiday."

"But, Angeline, isn't a child's place with her mother?"

"Judd will be good to her, I'm sure."

Angeline was crying, Lise was certain of it. "I can't believe he'd take her from you," she burst out.

"I have to believe it will be for the best," Angeline whispered.

"The man's heartless! Heartless and horrible."

"I don't want to fight him—there'd be so much publicity, and Emmy would be harmed by that."

"You're so generous," Lise exclaimed. "Poor little Emmy."

"Please, Lise, let's talk about something else," Angeline said, her voice quivering. "Have you seen the latest Donna Karan collection? I'm ordering one of everything—absolutely fabulous use of line and color."

"You're also very brave," Lise said forthrightly. "And yes, I did see an article in a magazine about her collection, rave reviews everywhere…"

With a jerk she came back to the present, to Marthe saying crossly, "Really, Lise, have you been listening to a word I've said?"

"I was thinking about Angeline," Lise said truthfully. "About how brave she was when Emmy went to Judd's custody."

"Judd!" Marthe spat. "He manipulated every one of his legal connections, and used to the hilt the fact that Angeline was moving to France. As if that would have made any difference to a three-year-old."

"I've met Emmy...she has Angeline's eyes," Lise said. "As you probably know, there was a fire three days ago at Judd's house—I was part of the crew."

Marthe clutched the arm of her chair with her arthritic, diamond-encrusted fingers. "Judd Harwood ruined my daughter's life. Once a month the child comes here for Sunday lunch, and that's all the contact I'm allowed."

One more strike against Judd, that he would keep his daughter from her grandmother as well as her mother. "Do you find Emmy shy?" Lise asked diplomatically.

"The child barely says a word. He's poisoned her against me, I know he has."

"How long since Angeline's seen her?"

"She finds it terribly painful to see her," Marthe replied. "Angeline was always so sensitive. As sensitive as she's beautiful." She gave Lise's casual attire and flaming curls a disparaging look. "It's unfortunate you didn't inherit the same looks, Lise. Of course my sister was no beauty."

Inwardly Lise winced; disparaging comparisons between her and her cousin had always been one of Marthe's themes. How could red hair and green eyes compare with Angeline's svelte blond elegance? She said lightly, "Well, we can't all be world-famous models, *Tante*."

"I'd hoped to go to France for Easter. But Angeline's put that visit off, something to do with Henri's schedule."

Marthe's mouth was a discontented line. "Perhaps she'll come this way instead," Lise suggested.

"She hasn't mentioned that as a possibility. But then she's so busy...three weeks ago she went to Monaco for a wedding, I have pictures here from one of the society magazines."

Marthe was an avid collector of clippings; obediently Lise admired the gathering of glossy aristocrats in their designer outfits. Angeline, as always, looked radiant; she was on the arm of an Italian newspaper magnate. "Henri was busy with the vineyard," Marthe sniffed. "Naturally Angeline never lacks for escorts—something Judd willfully misconstrued as infidelity." Viciously she dug her nails into the brocade arm of her chair. "As if Angeline would break her vows. And as if he were innocent in that respect. You have no idea what my poor daughter suffered from that man."

Judd no doubt kissed every woman as though there was no tomorrow, Lise thought painfully. Today he'd tried to tell her she was special; but the words meant nothing. His entire history mitigated against any such possibility. She said in a neutral voice, "He's very attractive."

"Angeline was so young when she met him. Young and impressionable. If I'd known then what I know now, I would never have allowed the match to happen."

Lise rather doubted this; Marthe had always given her daughter everything she wanted, and all those years ago there had been no doubt that Angeline wanted Judd. At thirteen, Lise had been quite acute enough to know that.

Luckily the maid entered the room with a silver tea tray, preventing Lise from following her train of thought; the conversation limped along, and half an hour later, Lise stood up to go. Marthe presented the same cool cheek, and with a feeling of strong relief, Lise started to walk home.

She needed the exercise; even more, she needed to exorcise Marthe's chronic discontent. But everything she'd learned today had only confirmed what she already knew:

Judd had treated his wife disgracefully. There wasn't a worry in the world that she herself would fall for him. Not again.

Her foot skidded on a patch of ice. Judd wasn't all bad, though. She would swear he loved Emmy. Unless he was a consummate actor, his pain and helplessness in the face of the little girl's nightmares had been all too real.

Stop thinking about him, Lise scolded herself. You'll never see him again and that's the way it should be. So get on with your life, and figure out what you're going to do next. Quit your job? Work in a bookstore? Take a veterinary assistant's course? Or spend all your savings to lie on a beach in the Caribbean and feel the sun on your face?

No way. She couldn't afford to do that.

When Lise finally reached her own street, the first thing she saw was Dave's battered Honda parked outside her apartment block. As she hurried into the lobby, he was pushing her buzzer. "Hi," she said warmly, pleased to see him; he was so uncomplicated, so straightforward after Judd.

He grinned at her; although she did notice with faint unease that he looked unusually tense. "I was just visiting my aunt," she added, "and decided to walk home."

"Want to go to the bistro for a bite?"

"Love to."

But when they were seated across from each other, twining the cheese from onion soup around their spoons, Lise said abruptly, "What's up? You don't seem yourself."

"I'm not. There's something I want to ask you."

His brown eyes looked at her without guile; but his fingers were clamped around his soup spoon as though it were an ax he might use to break down a door. "Go ahead," she said slowly.

"We've dated quite a bit, Lise. Gone to movies and

house parties, had meals together.'' He gazed at his whole wheat roll as if he wasn't quite sure what it was. ''I've kissed you good night. Sometimes we hold hands. But that's it. Something has always stopped me—''

''Dave, I—''

''No, let me finish.'' He looked up. ''You're off for the next few days and I've got five days' vacation I have to take before the end of March. Let's go away together, Lise. To a cabin in the Laurentians. To a fancy hotel in Quebec City. It doesn't really matter where. I just want to spend time with you.'' He covered her hand with his. ''I want to go to bed with you.''

Her lashes dropped to hide her eyes. Twice in one day, she thought in dismay, and wished with all her heart that Dave hadn't chosen tonight, of all nights, to break the silence of years. She gazed down at his hand. She could feel its weight, its warmth, of course she could. But she felt no desire to press it to her cheek, to trace the lines in his palm with her tongue. To hold it and never let go. If it had been Judd's hand…in a confused rush, she muttered, ''That's sweet of you. But—''

''I'm doing this all wrong,'' Dave announced. He suddenly stood up, came around to her side of the table and pulled her to her feet. Then he kissed her very thoroughly and with obvious enjoyment.

Lise stood still in his embrace, discovering within herself a strong urge to weep. Because she felt nothing. Absolutely nothing. Then Dave released her and stepped back. Someone gave a wolf whistle from one of the other tables. Ignoring it, Dave urged, ''Say yes, Lise. Please say yes.''

''I can't, Dave,'' she whispered. ''I just can't.''

''Why not? We can go away together, see what happens. No pressure, just spend some time with each other.''

She had to end this. ''I'm not in love with you,'' she

said desperately. "Not the least bit. So I can't go away with you, it would be wrong for both of us—I could never give you what you want."

She could feel the stillness in his body; his fingers were clamped around hers with something of the strength with which he'd hauled her through the burning window at Judd's house. Lise added with a weak smile, "Your soup's getting cold."

"You really mean it, don't you?" As she nodded unhappily, Dave demanded, "Is there someone else?"

"No!" How could she possibly tell him what happened to her when she came within ten feet of a man she despised? "I'm really sorry," she muttered. "But I know I'm right. You're my friend, Dave. And that's all I want."

Dave dropped his hands to his sides, sat down and automatically started to eat again. Lise sat down as well. Her shoulder was aching and she felt as though the day had gone on entirely too long. But she couldn't walk out on Dave; he deserved better than that. Valiantly she tried to talk about work and the snowstorm that was predicted, and when the waiter finally brought the bill, she could have cried with relief. Dave then drove her home. Pulling up outside her building, he said stiffly, "I'd rather we didn't date for a while. If it's all the same to you."

"So we won't be friends anymore?"

"Someday. Just not right now."

"I'm thinking of quitting the job anyway."

She hadn't meant to tell Dave that. He said incredulously, "*Quit?* What for? What else would you do?"

"I'm tired. I've done this job for ten years and I've had enough. I need a break. A rest."

"Good thing the rest of us don't feel that way."

She said more strongly, "Don't lay guilt trips on me, Dave, please. Look, I've got to go. Take care of yourself, won't you? And I'm truly sorry."

Before he could answer, Lise got out of his car and hurried indoors. By the time she'd opened the inner security door, Dave had driven away. She ran up the stairs to her floor, unlocked her apartment door, closed it behind her and sagged against it. She'd hurt Dave. A lot, by the look of his face. What was the matter with her? She couldn't respond to a good man who was dependable and brave; yet a man who manipulated those closest to him as though they were pieces on a chessboard had awoken her body to passion and hunger.

There was no sense in it. No sense whatsoever.

Lise woke the next morning to a leaden sky and a forecast for snow and freezing rain. In the cool morning light one fact seemed inescapable: she'd probably lost Dave's friendship last night. Which hurt. A lot.

One more reason to quit her job, she decided. The only bright spot in the day was that her shoulder felt better; nor was it quite so luridly hued. She'd phone a couple of friends to see if they were free for lunch; and then she'd go shopping. When the going gets tough, the tough go shopping: a motto Lise had always rather approved of. It beat taking aspirin.

After her shower, Lise pulled on her robe, which was full-length, made of fuchsia-colored fleece, and clashed with her hair. Fuchsia made a statement, she thought, grinning at herself in the mirror. Although maybe not a fashion statement. At least, not one Angeline would approve of.

Her hair, still damp, stood out in a cloud around her head. She'd buy a paper while she was out, and check the job market; she'd also phone the technology institute that ran the course to become a vet's assistant. What she wouldn't do was sit around bemoaning the loss of Dave…or think about Judd winging south with Emmy. No future in that.

Lise was cutting into a honeydew melon for breakfast when the doorbell rang. The knife slipped, slicing her index finger rather than the melon. She mouthed a very pungent word under her breath. Surely it wasn't Dave, hoping she'd changed her mind. Wrapping a wad of tissues around her hand, she went to the door. But her finger was bleeding rather profusely; trying to tighten the tissue, which was already splotched with red, she undid the latch and said, "Dave, I—oh. It's you."

"Yeah," said Judd, "it's me. What have you done to your finger?"

"It's only a cut."

In two seconds he was in the door, had deposited a suitcase on the floor, and was wrapping a pristine white handkerchief around her finger. Lise tried to pull free. "You'll ruin your handkerchief—don't make such a fuss!"

"Head for the bathroom," Judd ordered. "My turn to rescue you."

"I don't need rescuing," she retorted through gritted teeth. "And what are you doing here anyway?"

He said with a sudden, charming grin, "Oh, hadn't you guessed? I'm kidnapping you. Or, to be more accurate, Emmy and I are kidnapping you. She's waiting downstairs in the limo—we're on our way to the airport."

"Rich people don't do the kidnapping—they get kidnapped," Lise said peevishly, and allowed herself to be pulled in the direction of the bathroom, where in short order Judd taped her finger. He did it in a very businesslike manner; Lise concentrated her thoughts on ten-foot snowbanks and the Antarctic ice cap.

"There," he said. Then, taking his time, he surveyed her from head to foot. "You sure like bright colors."

She grimaced. "As a kid, I always inherited Angeline's

clothes. Pastels that looked fabulous on her and made me look like a sick puppy.''

With sudden violence Judd thrust his hands into the soft, tangled mass of her curls. ''We always come back to Angeline, don't we?'' he muttered. ''I'll tell you one thing—you're as different from her as fuchsia is from pale pink.'' Then he bent his head to kiss her, his tongue laving her lips, demanding entrance.

Lise stood as rigid as a post; and this time she thought about Angeline, and about Emmy sleeping in the attic because she was lonely for her father. Suddenly, with all her strength, she pushed away from Judd, wrenching her head free. How dare he take her for granted? Assume that she was panting to be kissed by him? ''Go to Dominica, Judd Harwood,'' she seethed. ''Or go to hell. I don't care where you go as long as you're out of this apartment in two seconds flat!''

''Go get dressed, Lise,'' he countered, and to her fury she saw that he was laughing at her. ''Anything'll do. Bring sunglasses.''

''You don't get it, do you? You just don't get it. I'm not going to Dominica with you!''

''You've got to. Emmy's expecting you.''

''Emmy doesn't care one way or the other what I do.''

''I asked her if she wanted you to come.''

''And what did she say?''

Judd hesitated, remembering the actual words of that conversation with unfortunate accuracy. ''Would you like Lise to go away with us, Emmy?'' he'd asked.

''If you want her to.''

''I'm asking about you. What you want.''

Emmy said elliptically, ''Her hair's really pretty.''

''It is, isn't it? She works hard at her job, Emmy, I'm sure she could do with a holiday.''

''She's nicer than Eleanor.''

Judd winced. He'd dated Eleanor, daughter of an earl, just long enough to discover she had ice water in her veins and disliked small children. "I think Lise liked you," he ventured, and received in return one of Emmy's silent, inscrutable looks.

He came back to the present; Lise was gazing at him just as steadily. He had no more idea what Lise was thinking than he'd had with Emmy, he thought in exasperation. He'd built a multimillion-dollar business from the ground up and he couldn't think what to say to a woman he barely knew? He opened his mouth and heard himself say, "Emmy wasn't what you'd call enthusiastic."

Lise said dryly, "For once, you're being honest."

"You deserve honesty," Judd said slowly, and knew he'd said something very profound. What the devil was going on? He didn't like subterfuge, but never before with a woman had he had this burning urge to avoid even the smallest of deceits. Lise looked a little disconcerted, he noticed. Good. If he was off balance, it wouldn't hurt for her to be, too.

"I'm not going," she said evenly, crossing her arms over her breasts. "Emmy won't be disappointed, and I'm sure you'll manage to find someone else."

"I don't want someone else. I want you."

"No way."

Judd held on to his temper. Taking her by the hand, he walked down the hallway toward the front door, where he undid the gleaming leather suitcase he'd brought with him. "I went shopping yesterday," he said. "For you."

"You mean you bought me clothes?" Lise demanded, her green eyes full of hostility.

"Yeah. Figured your wardrobe probably wasn't loaded with stuff suited for the tropics."

"How did you know what size?"

"I've held you in my arms, Lise."

She blushed scarlet, in interesting contrast to both her robe and her hair. Ignoring her flaming cheeks with a disdain he had to admire, she gave her head a defiant toss. "You're going to be busy when you get back from Dominica," she said. "Returning everything."

"Beachwear, a couple of nightgowns, shorts, tops and an outfit for dinner," he said equably. "But why would I bother returning them? I'll just keep them for the next woman who comes along. Right?"

"So you were planning on buying me?" Lise flashed. "Stick a few fancy clothes in a suitcase and she'll follow me anywhere? Panting like a puppy dog?"

"No," he said tightly. "That wasn't the plan. I can't buy you, Lise—you think I haven't figured that out yet?"

"I don't want your money. Or your clothes."

She was telling the truth, he thought in a great surge of exhilaration. It was a long time since he'd been wanted for himself. Not for his money, his possessions, or the power he wielded. He said the obvious. "You want me, though."

"Maybe I do. It's called lust. So what?"

"So come to Dominica with me and Emmy. Separate bedrooms, a private beach and a swimming pool, and no responsibilities."

"I can't, Judd," Lise said in sudden anguish. "That's not the way I operate. I'd be using you—don't you see?"

She meant every word she was saying and she wasn't playing hard to get; he'd stake his whole fleet of jets on that. Putting all the force of his personality behind his words, Judd said, "You saved Emmy's life, Lise. You might be forgetting that. I'm not. Three days in the sun—not much recompense for something that's beyond price."

Her eyes dropped before the blazing intensity of his to the suitcase open at his feet. Then she said in a strangled voice, "What's underneath that yellow thing?"

That yellow thing was a very expensive coverup for a

miniscule bikini. Judd knelt, pushing it aside to reveal a jade-green silk dress with cap sleeves, a plunging neckline and a long flare of skirt. "Quite by chance I saw it in the window of a boutique near Westmount Square. It seemed to belong to you—Lise, what's wrong?"

Her hands were clasped in front of her; tears glimmered in her eyes. Swiftly Judd stood up, taking her by the shoulders. "Don't you like it? It's just that I could picture you—"

Her words tumbled over one another. "I saw it, too. Last week. Before I met you. I was shopping one day, just wandering, and I saw it in the window and it was so beautiful and I knew I'd look wonderful in it, that it was made for me. I also knew I couldn't possibly afford it, and where would I wear it anyway? To the annual firefighters' dinner? To the drugstore? It was from another woman's life. Not mine." She shivered. "I—it scares me, Judd. That you saw it and bought it because you knew somehow that it belonged to me."

"Lise," Judd said harshly, "go put on jeans and a shirt. You're coming with us, and I swear I won't as much as lay a finger on you the whole time we're there. And when you get home, you can keep the dress—it's yours."

A tear slowly trickled down her cheek. She said raggedly, "I never cry. I can't afford to, too many awful things happen in my job and four or five of the guys would give their eyeteeth to see me behave like a typical female."

Judd ached to take her in his arms and kept his hands rigidly at his sides. "A few days away from your job," he said quietly, "that's all I'm giving you. That and a dress that'll make your eyes look like a tropical sea."

She scrubbed at her cheeks with the back of her hand. "I'll go and get ready," she muttered. "I won't be long."

With none of her usual grace, she scurried from the room. Judd watched her go. He'd said he wouldn't touch her; he had no idea how he was going to stick to that vow. But he'd have to keep his hands off her even if it killed him. Because he'd promised. Stooping to close the suitcase, he carefully tucked the dress away. He owed it a huge debt of gratitude; Lise had capitulated because of it.

He'd done some difficult things in his life. But he had the feeling that nothing would measure up to the challenge of staying out of Lise Charbonneau's bed.

CHAPTER FIVE

IT WAS evening. Judd was indoors putting Emmy to bed. Lise was sitting by herself on the tiled patio that overlooked the ocean, where the sun had set in barbaric splendor. The first stars were piercing a sky soft as velvet; the doves had fallen silent, and the brilliant magenta hues of the bougainvillea that clambered over the trellises had been swallowed by darkness. How long since she'd relaxed so completely in a setting so utterly beautiful? So luxurious?

Never.

She'd stepped outside her ordinary life the minute she'd climbed into Judd's limo outside her apartment. The uniformed chauffeur. The sleek private jet on the tarmac at Dorval, bearing the elegant logo of one of Judd's international airlines. And then, hours later, the arrival at the villa here on Dominica's east coast, the forested grounds opening to reveal a sprawling bungalow artfully constructed of native materials, its interior painted in tranquil pastels and open to the ocean breeze. Flowers everywhere, hibiscus and orchids and scarlet anthurium. Delicious meals that she, Lise, neither had to prepare nor clean up. She felt as though she were living in a dream, as though none of this was real.

Judd, so far, had been a perfect companion. Unobtrusively he'd made sure she had everything she needed, and he hadn't as much as laid one finger on her. He was keeping his promise.

A faint breeze stirred the palm trees, whose fronds clashed gently together like taffeta skirts. Lise stretched out a little more comfortably on the teak recliner, feeling the silk of her loose cream trousers slide against her thighs; her shirt was also silk, in a subtle shade of primrose yellow. Clothes Judd had chosen and paid for.

She should go to bed before he came back. Just in case his promise was an empty one and he planned to seduce her in this paradisiacal setting. Her lashes drooped to her cheek. She could trust him. Surely. It would be small thanks for saving Emmy's life were he to make love to her against her will.

Too sleepy to worry, too tired to remember how she'd fallen into his arms as easily as ripe mangoes fell from the trees on his estate, Lise closed her eyes. The soft gossip of the waves gentled any fears she might have had. Her breathing settled into a slower, deeper rhythm.

Ten minutes later Judd walked back out on the patio. It led from the spacious open-air dining room, which was edged with banks of purple and white orchids, toward the pool and the beach, so that house and sea were linked in a way that pleased him. Then he stopped short.

Lise had fallen asleep.

The golden light from the dining room angled across her face. Her hair glowed like a banked fire; her breasts rose and fell with her breathing. There were blue shadows under her closed lids, he noticed with a catch at his heart. Or at least he supposed it was his heart. How would he know? Other than Angeline, he'd never allowed the women in his life to affect him emotionally. No time to. No need to. No desire to.

His thoughts marched on. Today he'd gotten what he wanted: Lise here in his beloved Dominican retreat. For four nights. Yet in her apartment when he was trying to persuade her to come, he'd promised he wouldn't seduce her.

You're a goddamn fool. Why else did you invite her here?

Why else indeed? Gratitude, of course. But even that, deep though it went, seemed a pale force compared to his aching need to possess Lise. To make her his own in the most primitive way possible.

Lust. That's all it was. It was a long time since he'd been with a woman; and he certainly wasn't in love with her.

He'd fallen in love once, at the age of twenty-three, with Angeline. He could remember as if it were yesterday his first sight of her. He'd come out of the office tower in Manhattan where he'd been negotiating the purchase of four Boeing 737s, negotiations where he'd put his entire financial future on the line; as a result, adrenaline was racing through his veins. He'd crossed the street, glancing at the small crowd that had gathered on the sidewalk to watch a photo shoot, and then he'd seen her: an exquisite creature with a swath of straight blond hair and eyes of a midnight-blue. She was modeling a flared mink coat; diamonds blazed at her lobes and around her throat. Their eyes had met and he'd known instantly that he was going to marry her. That he wouldn't rest until he had.

Eventually they had married. But they hadn't lived happily ever after. Far from it.

Never again.

Lise stirred in her sleep. Her neck was crooked at an awkward angle; asleep, she looked both younger and more vulnerable. Less likely to bite his head off, he thought wryly. Yet wasn't her spirit one of the many things that drew her to him? Maybe tomorrow he'd see that Emmy had her supper early, and ask Lise to wear the green dress for dinner.

And then what? Leave her at the door of her room without as much as—his own words—laying a finger on her?

What had possessed him to make that promise, so easily spoken, so impossible to achieve? He was no saint, that he knew.

But for tonight, he'd better keep the promise.

He stooped and gathered Lise in his arms. She mumbled something under her breath. Then, in a way that made his heart thud in his chest, she curled into his body with a small sigh of repletion. The warmth of her cheek seared through his shirt; her fragrance drifted to his nostrils, hinting of a tangled garden filled with light-dappled flowers. And hummingbirds, he thought, remembering her T-shirt the day he'd cleaned up the spilled rice, the way it had hugged the curves of her breasts.

His face set, Judd stood up. Holding Lise in his arms, he marched across the patio and through the dining room. The bedrooms were angled to catch the trade winds; his was next to Lise's. As he pushed open the door to her room with his knee, inadvertently her elbow bumped the door frame. Her eyes jerked open, startled as a young bird's. He said quickly, "It's okay, you fell asleep and I was just—"

Her gaze had flown to the shadowed bedroom with its big bed heaped with soft pillows. She cried, "Judd, you promised!"

Swiftly he crossed the room and dumped her on the bed. "And I'm keeping that promise," he said through gritted teeth. "Don't you believe one word I say?"

Lise lurched to her feet, shoving her hands into her pockets. She'd been dreaming about Judd, the heat of his skin suffusing the dream, entwining her in its magic. And now here he was, his big body looming over hers to the soft whisper of the winds in the palm trees. Belatedly, she noticed something else: he didn't look the slightest bit interested in seducing her; he was far too angry for that.

Trying desperately to gather her wits, Lise said stiffly,
"I'm sorry, I jumped to conclusions."

"You sure did."

"I've apologized, Judd."

"Next time, try giving me the benefit of the doubt."

"There won't be a next time."

Judd's breath hissed between his teeth. "Damn right
there won't," he said, turned on his heel and marched
across the room, shutting the door behind him with exag-
gerated care. Lise stood very still. She wanted to scream
and yell. She wanted to pound the pillows until feathers
flew all over the room. She wanted Judd in her bed.

Slowly she sank down on the mattress, her eyes wide in
the darkness. The dream, she thought numbly. She was
simply trying to transpose a dream into reality. Or else her
judgment and coolheadedness were being destroyed by the
total sense of unreality that had taken hold of her in the
limo and stayed with her ever since she'd arrived in this
gorgeous retreat.

Of course she wasn't going to make love to Judd. She'd
made some mistakes in her life, but that would outdo them
all. Big time.

Judd had made a promise to her. Now she was making
one to herself. Don't make the smallest move to encourage
him. Treat him like a piece of furniture if that's what it
takes. But stay out of his bed and don't let him in yours.

Her fists were clenched in her pockets; she made a valiant effort to relax them. She'd be all right. Of course she
would. If she could handle a whole fire station full of men,
she could handle Judd Harwood. On which resolve Lise
stripped to her underwear, pulled the sheets to her chin
and eventually fell asleep.

At the breakfast table, which was shaded by vines hung
with big, lemon-yellow blossoms, Emmy made it clear she

wanted to spend the morning on the beach. "Sure," Judd said, adding easily, "bring your sunscreen, Lise, and wear a hat."

"Oh, I think I'll hang around on the patio and read."

He raised one brow. But all he said was, "The room across from my bedroom is a library—help yourself."

So Lise was settled in the same recliner when Judd and Emmy left for the beach. Judd in a pair of navy trunks took Lise's breath away; she dragged her eyes from the breadth of his tanned back, the taper of his waist, his long, tautly muscled legs. It wasn't fair, she thought wildly, burying her face in her book. No man should look that good.

But she was keeping her promise.

Unfortunately Emmy plunked herself down on the sand well within view of Lise. Which meant Lise had to watch the long curve of Judd's spine as he knelt beside Emmy building a sand castle; and then watch him cavorting in the waves with his daughter. She could have joined them. She didn't. But she did very soon throw her book down on the tiles with an exclamation of disgust, and go indoors to change into her bikini. At least she could work off some energy in the pool.

The bikini, chosen for her by Judd, comprised two scraps of yellow-flowered fabric that left very little to the imagination. Lise hauled her hair back with a ribbon, marched back outdoors and dived into the long, rectangular pool, which glittered turquoise in the sun. She began with a breaststroke that favored her sore arm, gradually working up to an overarm crawl as her muscles loosened in the warm, buoyant water. The exercise calmed her. After all, she could be back in Montreal, clinging to the fire truck as it careered through the icy streets. Anything was better than that. She darn well wasn't going to ruin this holiday just because of Judd Harwood. Or Judd Harwood's body.

Somersaulting at the near end of the pool, she pushed off, arrowing through the water with her eyes open. Then Emmy's body suddenly cannonballed into the pool in a swirl of bubbles. With a strong thrust of her left arm, Lise burst upward to the surface. Judd was in the pool, too, his slate-blue eyes laughing at her. "We're playing tag," he said. "You're it, Lise."

"I'm getting out now," she sputtered.

"Catch me if you can," Emmy yelled.

Emmy was laughing, too; she looked very different from the little girl huddled in terror in the far corner of an attic. Oh God, thought Lise, get me out of here, and swam toward the child as fast as she could. But at the last minute Emmy dove deep and suddenly Judd was beside Lise. "Bet you can't catch me," he teased.

Play it safe. Remember your promise.

Go for broke.

Lise lunged for him, but he twisted away from her, splashing water in her face. With a vengeful cry she went after him, slicing through the water, angling so she headed him toward one corner of the pool. At the last minute she dove and touched him on the knee before streaking to the very bottom of the pool. Then he was swimming alongside her, his body wavering in the rippled light. Swiftly he stroked closer and kissed her hard on the mouth; her eyes still wide-open, she watched him rise to the surface.

Badly out of breath, Lise pushed off from the bottom, gulping in mouthfuls of air when she reached the surface. In a flurry of spray she set off in pursuit of Emmy. Even under eight feet of water, she'd loved being kissed by Judd. Technically, of course, he still hadn't broken his promise. He'd only touched her with his lips. Not with his fingers.

Twenty minutes later all three of them climbed out of

the pool. Lise said breathlessly, "That was fun—you're a good swimmer, Emmy."

Emmy gave Lise one of her level looks. "Dad taught me," she replied and reached for her towel.

It wasn't so much what Emmy said, Lise thought ruefully, but how she said it: as though she were closing a door in your face. Judd said casually, "Here, have a towel."

Water was trickling down his chest, his body hair slick to his skin. The curve of his rib cage, the hollow at the base of his throat, his narrow hips: he entranced her, Lise thought helplessly, grabbed for the towel and buried her face in it. Stay away from him. Ignore him. Pretend he's a chair by the side of the pool.

What a laugh.

Sally, who ran the kitchen, had put glasses of guava juice and a plate of roti and sliced pineapple on the teak table that was shaded by a huge beach umbrella near the pool house; further shade was cast by tulip trees and palms. Lise hauled the yellow coverup over her head and sat down, discovering that she was ravenous and that her shoulder felt not too bad at all. Judd told a couple of very amusing stories about flights he'd monitored in the early days of his airline company; not to be outdone, Lise described some of the trees she'd climbed to rescue cats who hadn't wanted rescuing. And all the while she was aware of Judd watching her, of his eyes on her shoulders, her breasts, her thighs. He was very discreet; Emmy, she was sure, had no inkling of what he was doing. But she, Lise, knew. She felt as though he were undressing her. As though his eyes were stroking her as tangibly as his long, lean fingers would explore her flesh.

He wasn't laying a finger on her. Yet she felt seduced. She ate the last crumb of roti on her plate and finished her juice. Then she said brightly, "I'm going to have a nap. See you both later."

"Sleep well," Judd said blandly.

Lise hurried across the tiles in what was unquestionably a retreat. She showered in her luxuriously appointed bathroom, dried her hair, then lay down on the bed, wearing one of the two nightgowns Judd had chosen. Silk, again, sensual as a caress. Certain she was too keyed up to sleep, Lise closed her eyes; and opened them to the low slant of sunlight through the louvered windows.

She'd slept for nearly five hours. Quickly she got up, dressing in the same pants and top she'd worn last night; they covered her more completely than any of the other garments Judd had chosen. Then she ventured out into the hallway. Emmy and Judd were sitting on the patio, playing checkers, and for a moment she observed them from the shadows. There was an ease between them, she thought painfully. A connection that was very real. Judd, in other words, was a good father.

This didn't fit Angeline's description of him as an absentee father who had snatched his daughter away from her mother from motives of revenge and control. Or had Angeline simply implied all that, and Lise herself had filled in the gaps?

He couldn't fake being a good father. Certainly not with a child as astute as Emmy. Lise backed further into the shadows, then fled toward the library with its polished rosewood shelving, where she curled up in a deliciously comfortable bamboo chair and did her best to concentrate on the words on the page. She felt both lonely—or was excluded a more accurate word?—and frightened. She didn't like either emotion.

Half an hour later, Judd came looking for her. Dressed in cotton shorts and a T-shirt, his hair ruffled, he stationed himself in the doorway. "What's up, Lise?" he said roughly. "What—or who—are you hiding from?"

"I'm not hiding! I'm reading."

"Dinner's ready."

"Fine. I'll be right along."

"Don't wait for me, in other words," he said with dangerous quietness.

"I need to brush my hair, put on some lipstick."

"You don't need either one—you're one hundred percent gorgeous just as you are."

Lise stood up, smiling in spite of herself. "You can stroke my ego anytime you like."

"Don't you *know* how beautiful you are?"

"Angeline's beautiful. I'm average."

Judd ran his fingers through his hair. "Who told you that?"

"Marthe. Over and over again, while I was growing up."

Judd said a very rude word under his breath. "Do something for me, will you? Repeat five times a day, *I'm a beautiful woman. Judd says so.* Got it?"

"But I'm not sophisticated! Or elegant."

"You're real," he said.

Lise swallowed hard. He meant it. Temporarily speechless, her throat tight, she heard him add, "There's something else. You slept for five hours this afternoon—you're exhausted, aren't you?"

"I'm not used to the heat."

He gave her a scathing look. "Give me a break. You're worn-out, you think I can't see that? So I've got a proposition for you. We'll talk about it this evening after Emmy's in bed."

"No proposition you can mention could possibly interest me and you sure are good at giving orders."

"I didn't get where I am by letting people walk all over me. So don't try it."

Her temper rising, Lise said, "I'll do what I damn well please."

"You're pushing your luck, sweetheart."

"Don't call me that!"

"I don't mean it literally—trust me."

She didn't know which was worse, his high-handedness or his sarcasm. In a voice smooth as cream, she said, "You did mention dinner, didn't you?"

"I pity the guys who have to share the fire truck with you," Judd said pithily.

Brushing the petals of the bronze lilies in a bowl on the table, an involuntary smile curving her mouth, Lise said, "Fire truck—what fire truck? It all seems a million miles away."

"Good," said Judd. "Then I've achieved something at least."

Lise bit her lip. "I'm really grateful to be here, Judd, please don't misunderstand me. And yes, I'm tired. But it's more than that. I don't want to get involved with you— even assuming you were willing, which I doubt. My life and yours are miles apart, and that's the way they've got to stay. So if I'm keeping a certain distance between us, I'm acting out of self-preservation, that's all."

He stepped nearer. "You speak your mind, don't you?"

"Saves trouble in the long run."

"You sure are different from any other woman I've ever met. And yes, I'm including Angeline," Judd said with suppressed violence.

He was standing so close she could see the dark curl of his lashes, and the curved line of his lower lip, so cleanly sculpted, so infinitely desirable. She wanted to run her fingertip along it. As her heart rate quickened, Judd grated, "I have no idea why I made that ridiculous promise."

"I made one, too. If it's any help," she said with a faint grin. "To keep my hands off you."

Twin devils danced in his eyes. "Did you indeed? But by mutual agreement promises can be broken."

"No, they can't! We're totally wrong for each other and I've never indulged in casual sex."

"Casual wasn't exactly what I had in mind," Judd responded. "And now, since Sally the cook is almost as quick-tempered as you, we'd better head for the dining room."

That was something else she'd noticed in the last twenty-four hours: the mutual respect between Judd and his employees. "You're very good with your staff," she said reluctantly.

"I'm not an ogre!"

Just the sexiest man I've ever laid eyes on. But fortunately Lise hadn't said that. Walking around him, she headed for the dining room.

After dinner Judd put Emmy to bed; then he and Lise played chess out on the patio. At five minutes after midnight, he said, lightly, "Checkmate."

"Ouch," said Lise, "I should have blocked your bishop two moves ago."

"You play well."

"Stephan taught me—one of my buddies on the night shift. It's a good way to stay awake." She gave him a limpid smile. "As I'm not on the night shift now, I'm going to bed. Good night."

As she pushed back her chair, he got up. "You notice I haven't mentioned my proposition," he said lazily. "I've decided to save it for later."

"Good for you," she responded amiably. "Saves us having another fight...I'm all for that."

"There's more than one way to avert a fight." His hands at his sides, Judd leaned forward and kissed her full on the mouth, a leisurely kiss of devastating intimacy. His tongue traced her lips; then he moved to her cheekbones, her closed lids, the long line of her throat. From a long way away Lise heard him murmur her name.

She felt boneless, weightless, ravaged by hunger, yet fed as she'd never been fed before. Nor had he laid a finger upon her. Frantically Lise drew back, her eyes like dark pools under the tropic sky. "No, Judd, please…"

"Just kissing you good night."

Her nipples were thrusting against her silk shirt; her whole body felt on fire. "Don't play games with me," she begged. "I'm not in your league, don't you see?"

"I kissed you because I wanted to. And you stayed because you wanted to. Admit it, Lise."

His eyes seemed to drill their way through her skull. "Wanted?" she cried. "I had no choice!"

With a whimper of pure distress, she whirled and ran for her room. She shut the door and jammed a fragile rattan chair under the handle, a ruse that couldn't possibly keep Judd out were he determined to enter, but which made her feel minimally better. One kiss and she was a basket case, she thought despairingly. Never in her life had she responded to a man the way she did with Judd.

She now understood why she'd never gone to bed with Dave. But years ago, when she was new at the job, she'd fallen in love with a firefighter from another district in Montreal, and had had a short-lived affair with him. The sex hadn't been great, even to someone of her very limited experience; and the ending of the affair, when he'd discovered that her address in Outremont didn't mean that she had old family money, could have been farcical if it hadn't been both humiliating and hurtful.

In the years that followed, the men she occasionally dated always got discouraged, sooner or later, by her dedication to a demanding and dangerous job with irregular hours. That was fine by her; her affair had destroyed something in her, a quality of trust that wasn't easily reestablished.

It was still fine by her, she thought fiercely. Meeting Judd hadn't changed anything. On which not entirely truthful conclusion, Lise managed to get to sleep.

The next day Lise, Judd and Emmy took off for the day, buying some lovely Carib baskets in Roseau, Dominica's charming capital, then walking to Trafalgar Falls, where they swam in the pool at its foot. They were home in time for dinner; Lise went to bed early. No chess game. No kisses under a velvet sky. No proposition. Whatever that meant.

Their final day, they hiked into the national park in the northern sector of the island. Lise loved the rain forest, so entangled, so deeply green, so shadowed by the huge buttressed chataignier trees. It smelled damp and fecund, and the small brightly colored birds that flickered through its branches entranced her.

Judd carried Emmy on his shoulders a lot of the way; Emmy, Lise knew, had not had a single nightmare since they'd arrived on the island. If Angeline had been wrong about Judd's capabilities as a father, had she also misled Lise about other facets of his life?

This was a new thought for Lise. She'd learned something else as well: that Judd could keep a promise. He had indeed not laid a finger on her the last two days. In fact, he'd withdrawn today in a way she could scarcely pinpoint yet knew to be real. She should have been relieved. She wasn't. Rather, his casual manner toward her made her intensely irritable. Perhaps he'd decided she wasn't worth the trouble. After all, the world must be full of women who'd fall into bed with him at the slightest encouragement.

One thing was clear, though: Judd had made her a promise and he'd kept it.

For whatever the reason.

When they got back to the villa, Emmy was packed off to bed with supper on a tray. Although she'd been nothing but polite to Lise the last three days, a few times Lise had caught the little girl simply staring at her, as though trying to fathom her; yet Lise felt no closer to her than she had when they'd set out. What had Judd told Emmy about the custody battle? Maybe he'd implied that Angeline didn't want her own daughter; which would explain Emmy's hesitancy to trust another woman. Or maybe, Lise thought more cynically, there'd been so many women in Judd's life that Emmy no longer bothered.

Her last dinner on the island. Tomorrow they were flying back to Montreal, to winter and normality, to her next shift at the fire station. Her bruises had faded beneath her carefully acquired tan; she was fit enough to go back to work. A prospect that gave her very little joy.

She opened her closet door. The jade-green dress was hanging there; she had yet to wear it. Smoothing the fabric with her fingers, she laid the dress on the bed, then spent the better part of five minutes staring at it in much the same way that Emmy had stared at her. Judd buying this dress had brought Lise to his villa. So was she going to leave without wearing it? Was she going to opt for the safe cream trousers and yellow shirt once again?

Was she a woman or a mouse?

Lise rummaged in her own suitcase for her prettiest underwear and her gold sandals. Then she made up her face with care, painted her toenails and fastened gold hoops to her earlobes. Finally she eased her body into the jade silk, linking its gold chain link belt around her waist.

The mirror showed her a stranger, a lissome creature with a cloud of red curls, whose eyes reflected the glorious hue of a garment that clung at hip and waist and breast. She looked sensual. Voluptuous. Available. Oh, no, thought Lise, I can't wear this.

A tap came at her door. "Dinner is served, missie."

It was Sally's assistant, who came from Roseau. "I'll be right there, Melanie," Lise called, closing her eyes in panic. How could Judd construe her appearance as anything other than the most blatant of invitations? Yet intuitively he'd chosen for her an outfit she'd longed—hopelessly—to possess.

Dammit, she was going to wear it. Even if walking into the dining room would require more courage than facing a three-alarm blaze. Squaring her shoulders, Lise left her room.

CHAPTER SIX

JUDD was gazing out at the darkened beach over the ledge of orchids in the dining room; because there was a local festival in town that evening, Sally and her assistant had the rest of the night off, and dinner had been served buffet-style on the vast mahogany sideboard. Emmy was already asleep. Perfect timing for seduction, he thought savagely. A seduction that wasn't going to happen. All he had to do was keep that goddamned promise for one more night and then he'd be home free.

Out of sight, out of mind? Would that work where Lise was concerned? He wasn't so sure. But it was worth a try.

What other option did he have?

A whisper of footsteps crossed the tiled floor. Alerted to Lise's presence, Judd turned around; his smile of welcome froze to his lips. For the space of five seconds he was struck dumb. Then he walked around the corner of the table, stopping only a few inches away from her and letting his gaze wander over her from head to foot. Her bare, rounded arms and creamy throat. The jut of her breasts and gentle indentation of her waist, clasped in gold. The smooth swell of her hips. Only when his eyes came back to her face did he realize that she was panic-stricken, the pulse fluttering at the base of her throat, and her spine rigid. Her expression that of a woman who knows she should be anywhere but where she was.

Clearing his throat, he said huskily, "To tell you you're beautiful is meaningless. Yet what else can I tell you? I—hell, Lise, I don't know what to say."

To his horror he saw that tears were glittering in her

eyes. Her temper he rather relished; her tears pierced all his defences. Because she'd told him she never cried? Craving to put his arms around her from the simple need to comfort her, knowing that if he did so he would have broken his promise, Judd stood still, his arms taut at his sides. He'd made that promise with very little thought for the consequences and as a means of getting Lise here to his villa: a manipulative promise, he thought stringently. But somehow over the last few days it had come to mean something. He had to keep it. For her sake and for his. And what the devil that meant, he didn't know. Didn't even want to know.

Lise was watching him, her face as unreadable as Emmy's. Then she drew a deep breath and reached out, taking his right hand in hers and very deliberately bringing it to rest on her shoulder. She said unsteadily, "All four fingers on me. How about that?"

His heart was pounding in his chest like a drum. Lise was releasing him from his promise...what else could her gesture mean? Judd said hoarsely, "Lise, I—are you sure?"

"No. Maybe. Oh God, I don't know."

As always, her honesty knocked him off balance. Angeline, so he'd come to understand, had never lied to him wittingly; she'd simply adjusted the truth to suit her needs in the moment. At first, very much in love, he'd made allowances for this. Later, as the months and years passed, he'd lost the ability to trust her; and had come to realize that trust was the essential foundation for love.

He said clumsily, "You always tell the truth, Lise, don't you? You blurt it out. You throw it in my face. Or you simply say it. Because that's how you live your life."

She didn't pretend to misunderstand him. "Not much room for lies when you're searching for a child who's lost in smoke and flames."

He flinched. Then, in a voice he scarcely recognized as his own, he asked the obvious. "Why did you put my hand on your shoulder?"

"Why did I wear this dress?"

"Two unanswerable questions?"

"You kept your promise—don't think I didn't notice. That's got something to do with it."

"Yeah...that crazy promise came to mean something. Something important."

Briefly she looked terrified out of her wits; he could feel her shrinking from him beneath his fingertips. "I could always plead temporary insanity," she faltered. "Maybe that's the only reason that makes any sense."

With a muffled groan Judd took her in his arms, and was instantly and achingly aware of the slenderness of her waist and the warmth of her hips, of the way her breasts brushed his shirtfront. He wanted with all the impulsions of his sexuality to make love to her as she'd never been made love to before. To ravish her, delight her, give her the most intense pleasure he was capable of. Don't, Judd, he thought ferociously. Don't go there! She's starting to trust you because you've kept a promise. Don't blow it. Not now. She deserves better than that.

Pulling back, he said roughly, "Lise, we'd better eat."

He felt her sudden stillness; she was staring at his shirt as if she'd never seen a row of buttons before. With careful politeness, she said, "Yes. You're right. Of course."

"If we don't," he said, "you know what's going to happen?"

This time a shiver ran through her. "Yes," she said in a low voice.

The emotion Judd felt now was undoubtedly tenderness. For him a totally new emotion, one that not even Angeline in those early days—and nights—had called up. There'd always been something detached about Angeline, a portion of herself kept firmly to herself; only later had he wondered if that had been part of her fascination for him: that he could never quite reach her core, no matter how hard he tried.

Run, he thought. Run for your life, buddy. Because if you make love to this red-haired woman, you'll never be the same again. You know that. And maybe she knows it, too. You don't want that kind of involvement. You swore off it years ago.

He moved away from her so that her hand fell to her side and said with a lightness that sounded almost genuine, "Sally will have my hide if we don't make at least an inroad into the food she's prepared. You haven't seen Sally on the warpath—not much puts the fear of God in me, but she sure does."

"Do I scare you, Judd?" Lise asked.

Of all the questions she could have asked, she'd chosen the one that was the most impossible to answer. He'd given enough away already by keeping that stupid promise. That's all you're getting, Lise Charbonneau, Judd thought. No more involvement. No, ma'am. Definitely not part of my game plan. He said coolly, "Other than Sally, I don't let women scare me."

Her lashes flickered. Then she lifted her chin; her courage stabbed him to the heart. "I get the message," she said. "So what's for dinner? And did Emmy go to sleep all right? She hasn't had any nightmares at all, has she? It was a good idea to bring her here, it's easy to see how much she loves the place. Not that I'm surprised, it's so beautiful."

Lise wasn't normally a chatty woman; her ability to be comfortable with silence was something else he'd noticed about her. He'd noticed a lot, Judd thought grimly, and said, "Cold pumpkin soup. A conch salad, plantain, curried shrimp, Creole pork chops…want me to go on?"

"Sounds wonderful," Lise said, with a smile that didn't quite reach her eyes.

The next hour Judd would long remember as one of the most excruciating in his life. He and Lise were painstakingly polite to each other, each talked at length about totally impersonal subjects, and they ate as though appeasing Sally were all that mattered. But finally they'd finished the sliced mangoes cooked in a ginger syrup, and had drained delicate china demitasses of coffee. Lise said with an artificial yawn, "I think I'll say good night, Judd, we have a long day ahead of us tomorrow."

"Sleep well," he said with just the right touch of detachment, and watched her leave the room. A few moments later he heard the decisive click of her bedroom door. Only then did he let his breath out in a long sigh.

You're a fool, Judd Harwood. You had your chance and you blew it. You could have bedded her. Gotten her out of your system.

A little voice sneered in his head, You figure one night with Lise would cure whatever's wrong with you? Now that really does make you a fool.

Come off it. She's just a woman. And I'm not in love with her, nowhere near.

You want me to list all her attributes? Starting with courage and ending with passion?

Oh, shut up, Judd thought irritably, and got up from the table. He carried the uneaten food back to the kitchen, storing it in the refrigerator; he blew out the candles; he checked on Emmy, who was sprawled across her bed fast asleep. There was no sound from Lise's room. Cursing himself, Judd went to his own room, had a shower that he tapered off to cold, with no noticeable effect, and pulled on the briefs that were all he wore to bed. Then he gathered a stack of articles he'd been meaning to read for the last two weeks, and tried to concentrate.

Angeline had never slept in this bed. She'd wanted the trendy islands where the jet set gathered, where there were casinos and nightclubs. Not peaceful Dominica with its dark sands and sleepy little capital. The only woman he'd ever brought here was Lise.

He wasn't going to think about Lise. Tomorrow he'd drop her off at her apartment and that would be that. Luckily Emmy had kept her guard up; he didn't need that further complication. His jaw tight, Judd picked up a pen and started jotting down notes.

Two hours later, he'd managed to whip up a half-decent level of concentration on an article about rising jet fuel costs. His brow furrowed, he quickly numbered the main points of the argument. Then a sudden, bitten-off cry of terror ripped the peaceful night air; his pen skidded on the page and he raised his head, like an animal sensing danger.

Emmy. Another nightmare.

Not bothering to pull on any clothes, Judd was out of bed in one quick movement and was running down the hallway. But as he flung open his daughter's door, he saw that Emmy was peacefully asleep, her arm thrown over Plush.

It hadn't been Emmy who'd screamed. So it must have been Lise.

He didn't bother tapping on Lise's door. Shoving it open, hearing it swing shut behind him, Judd said urgently, "Lise—what's wrong?"

Her voice quavered across the room. "S-something landed on the b-bed."

As he switched on the light, the biggest lizard he'd ever seen scurried across the bedclothes to the floor and vanished under the bed. With a gasp of horror, Lise cowered against the head of the bed. Judd sat down on the bed and started to laugh.

Shuddering, she sputtered, "It ran across my f-face and

woke me up—shut up, Judd, it's not the slightest bit funny!''

He laughed all the harder. ''You can enter burning buildings and deal with car wrecks, and a lizard makes you scream? Oh Lise, I've found your feet of clay.''

''You try it! Claws clinging to your cheeks and it's so damn dark you can't see your fingers in front of your face—Judd, will you please stop laughing?''

She was sitting up straight now, the covers around her waist, her hair a wild tangle around her furious face. He said, ''They get in through the louvers. If it's any comfort, the lizard was probably much more scared than you.''

''It's no comfort whatsoever.''

And suddenly Judd became aware that he was sitting on Lise's bed clad in nothing but a pair of briefs; and even more aware of the creamy rise and fall of her breasts in her silk nightgown. When he'd purchased it, he'd pictured it clinging to her body in all the right places. It clung all right, he thought, his mouth dry; and did what he'd been craving to do ever since he'd first seen Lise lying semi-conscious in a hospital bed in Montreal. Leaning forward, he took her by the shoulders, his fingers clasping her warm skin with acute pleasure. Then he kissed her upturned face, exposing all his fierce hunger for her. It was a kiss that seemed to go on forever. A kiss, he thought dimly, that she was more than returning.

Her arms were around his neck; her breasts were pressed to his bare chest. In passionate gratitude he felt her open to the thrust of his tongue, her own tongue playing with his with an eroticism that made his head swim. Lise wanted him. Wanted him as badly as he wanted her.

Had he ever doubted that?

Judd buried his hands in the silky mass of her hair, his lips sweeping the curve of her cheekbones; as he did so, the fragrance of her skin filled his nostrils. He pushed

down the thin straps of her gown, kissing her collarbone
and the gentle hollow of her throat. Then he found the firm
rise of her breast; his heart thudding against his rib cage,
Judd cupped its weight, teasing her nipple to hardness. Lise
moaned his name, her palms splayed against his chest, her
fingers playing with his body hair in a way that inflamed
him. He kissed her again, straining her to him, knowing
there was nowhere on earth he would rather be than in
Lise's bed. With Lise.

Her gown fell to her waist. He dropped his head to the
sweet valley between her breasts, kissing first one ivory
curve of flesh, then the other, feeling her fingers in his
hair, tracing the hard lines of his skull. Raw need over-
coming all caution, he pushed back the covers, twisting to
lie down and drawing her down beside him. "Take off
your gown, Lise—I want you naked."

With only a trace of shyness, she pulled the blue silk
over her head and threw it to one side. Judd pushed up on
one elbow, drinking in the soft arc of her waist and swell
of hip, the darker tangle of hair at the juncture of her
thighs, the slender length of each leg all the way to the
arch of her instep. He was not a man normally at a loss
for words. "Lise, you're exquisite," he said huskily.

She said, scarlet-cheeked, "No fair, Judd—you're still
dressed. Sort of."

He was also fully aroused, as she must be aware. He
yanked off his briefs, tossing them to the floor. "Come
here," he said; and then for the space of several minutes
said nothing else. His intent silence was broken only by
Lise's small gasps of delight, gasps that turned to broken
cries as he found the wet pink petals of flesh between her
thighs, teasing them open, stroking them with nothing but
an impassioned desire to bring her as much pleasure as he
could.

She threw back her head, writhing beneath his touch,

whimpering his name over and over again; as the tension gathered in her body, she held onto him with all her strength, her green eyes drowning in sensation. Then suddenly she was overwhelmed by the inexorable rhythms of release, her cries echoing in his ears as he held her close. The frantic hammering of her heart was as his own. Feeling as though he held the whole world in his arms, Judd murmured, "Lise...Lise, you're so incredibly beautiful."

Her face was pushed into his shoulder. "I—I never knew it could be so sudden. So powerful."

"And it's not over yet," he said, running his hand down the long curve of her back and drawing her closer to his erection. "We've only just begun."

She looked up, her irises shining like emeralds, laughter sparking their depths. "So I see," she said, and gave a sudden thrust of her hips toward him.

He gasped with pleasure. Then he felt her fingers encircle him, stroking the taut length of his penis. As his face convulsed, he muttered, "Keep that up and you're in trouble."

"Another promise?" she said hopefully.

"Yeah, it's a promise," he growled. "And I'm going to keep it. Kiss me, Lise."

She offered her lips with a generosity that touched him to the core. Then, infinitely seductive, she moved down his body, tasting his skin, laving his nipples with her tongue, and tracing the hard angle of one hipbone. "I love your body," she whispered, taking him in her hands again and caressing him until Judd wondered if he could die of pleasure.

Before he could lose control, he lifted her to straddle him. She slid over him, enclosing him in wetness and heat. In intimacy, he thought, pulling strands of her vivid hair to lie over the tilt of her breasts, and watching the play of expressions on her face. She was hiding nothing, he knew that. And would not have wanted it otherwise.

She rode him with fierce concentration, her knees braced on either side of his body, her breasts gently bouncing. He took her by the waist, loving the smoothness of her skin and her agility, aware through every nerve ending of the primitive building of impulsions older than time.

He wanted her closer, her face so near that he could see every change of expression. Holding her so that he stayed locked within her, Judd pulled her down, rolling over so that she was on her back and he covering her body with his own. He could lose himself in the green depths of her eyes, he thought. Lose himself and find himself? Find a man he scarcely knew? He said impetuously, "Hold me, Lise. Move with me."

"Oh, Judd..." she whispered, her irises deep pools of tenderness as she brushed her breasts against his body hair, back and forth with a delicious sensuality that spiked his hunger for her until it was all-consuming.

He thrust deep inside her, aware with every fiber of his being of her involuntary response. "Tell me you want me," he demanded. "Tell me, Lise."

She locked her arms around his waist and kissed him with passionate intensity, nibbling at his lips as she whispered, "I want you more than I can say. I want—oh, Judd, now. Please, now."

He was more than ready. Seized by his body's primitive rhythms, yet never so swept up that he lost sight of her face drowned in rapture, Judd cried out her name, again and again. Then, to his infinite gratification, he sensed her own pulsations, echoing his own: and heard her cries mingle with his. Fused, drained, at one with her with a completion that was unlike any union he'd ever known, Judd emptied within her. And wondered if he would ever be entirely separate from her again.

His forehead fell to her shoulder. His throat heaving, his heart trying to force its way out of his chest, he clung to her as if he were the one who was drowning. She said softly, "Judd, are you all right?"

And how was he supposed to answer that, when a love-making he hadn't planned had taken him to a place he'd never been before? "Complicated question," he muttered. "You sure know how to ask 'em."

"Yes or no will do," she murmured.

Alerted by something in her voice, Judd looked up. "My turn. Are you okay?"

"I feel—" Lise hesitated, then added in a rush, "I feel almost as though I was a virgin, someone who'd never made love before…I guess there aren't any words, Judd." With one hand, she smoothed the hair back from his sweat-damp forehead; and with a sudden tightness in his chest, he saw that her fingers were trembling.

He took her hand in his, kissing the backs of her knuckles. "Let's not try for words, then."

He drew her down to his shoulder, and closed his eyes; slowly the tumult in his body subsided and he became aware of himself again as a separate entity. As a man who definitely didn't want to try for words. After all, didn't that suit him right down to the ground? He didn't want to say things in the heat of the moment that he'd then be required to live up to. Women always took what you said to the bank. He didn't want commitment. Ever again. Freedom was the name of the game. Independence. It was the way he'd lived his life ever since his divorce, and just because a woman with hair like flame and a body that ravished all his senses had burst into his life didn't mean he had to change anything.

All the more reason not to change.

Burying his face in her throat, Judd said, "You're one heck of a woman, Lise Charbonneau."

There was the smallest of pauses before she said pertly, "Why, thank you. You're quite the guy yourself."

"I'm going to set up a one-man society for the preservation of lizards."

As he'd hoped, this made her laugh. "Yuk," she said.

He wrapped his arms around her and discovered something else: that he still wanted her. That there were a myriad ways of making love to her he hadn't tried yet, and even the thought of them turned him on. Get her out of his system? Who was he kidding? Maybe the lizard hadn't done him a favor after all, Judd thought grimly. If he'd had any smarts, he'd have stuck to his promise.

"What are you thinking?" Lise whispered.

Her face was clouded with uncertainty in a way that hurt Judd deep inside. To hell with caution, he thought. Right now her happiness was more important than a few niggling doubts. And why should he be so afraid of commitment? The word hadn't even been mentioned between him and Lise. Besides, hadn't he always taken what he wanted? "Can't you tell what I'm thinking?" he asked, easing a little closer to her. "Although I'm not sure my thought processes have much to do with it. Are you interested in a repeat?"

Her chuckle was full of mischief. "I suspect I could be persuaded."

"Good," said Judd, and set about to do just that, using all his skills of imagination and empathy.

The thing he hadn't quite counted on was how Lise met him more than halfway, with a generosity and abandon that aroused him to a fever pitch. Images of her spilled through his brain: the fullness of her breasts, swollen from his kisses; the tightness of her thighs, wrapped around him; the long curve of her spine, the wonderment in her emerald eyes as he caressed every inch of her body, committing it to memory in spite of his own best intentions. She was his, all his and only his, was his last thought before she tumbled into the abyss of release, pulling him with her every step of the way.

Overwhelmed by the sheer physicality of sensation, aware of being flooded by an uncomfortable blend of tenderness, protectiveness and terror, Judd held her close, and with a distant part of his brain wondered how he was going to say goodbye to her tomorrow. Goodbye? More like hello, he thought with another of those surges of fear. How often did a man and woman mate with such total involvement? Such a blissful satiation of needs and desires?

He had to get of here.

But Lise's head was resting on his chest, her hair tumbling over his rib cage in glorious abandon. Against his belly he could feel the racing of her heart; her breath wafted his skin. So what was he going to do? Tell her he was leaving right now because he was frightened out of his wits? He was a grown man, for God's sake. Men weren't supposed to be scared of women. Anyway, it took a lot to scare him.

Judd lay still and imperceptibly felt her breathing slip into the rhythms of sleep. So the choice was made: he had to stay. For now.

Was he going to say goodbye tomorrow? Is that what he wanted? If he were smart, that's what he'd do. He wasn't into commitment. Whereas Lise, he suspected, was the kind of woman to play for keeps.

Deadlock.

Did he want to hurt her? Surely not. Or was it already too late? So should he hurt her now, rather than later?

How was he going to drop her off at her apartment door and go home to his celibate life as if last night had never happened? This was the payoff for breaking promises, Judd thought caustically. And suddenly remembered his proposition, the one he hadn't yet broached to her. In theory, it was for Emmy's benefit. But in practice, it would certainly affect him.

With aching clarity he remembered something else: how ardently and trustingly Lise had opened to him, offering him unstintingly all the gifts of her body. Was he going to throw them back in her face? He gave an impatient sigh. He was known throughout the business world for making momentous decisions with the rapidity of gunfire; yet when it came to Lise, he felt immobilized by doubts and second thoughts and then still more doubts.

Keep your proposition to yourself, Judd Harwood. Goodbye is just a two-syllable word.

CHAPTER SEVEN

LISE woke to the soft cooing of doves in the jacaranda trees outside her room. Automatically she reached for Judd; but found only tangled sheets and a pillow. Her eyes flew open. She was alone, she thought in confusion. Alone and naked in her own bed.

Her skin smelled of his, her body suffused with a delicious languor; she hadn't dreamed their lovemaking. It had been real, wondrously and heart-wrenchingly real.

Where was he?

Emmy. Of course he couldn't stay in bed with Lise and risk his daughter finding them there together. But couldn't he have woken her before he left? Held her close and kissed her before leaving her alone?

Her nightgown was still lying on the floor, startlingly blue against the pale tile; and a hundred memories flooded Lise's mind. She'd had to travel all the way to a small tropical island to learn how powerful and utterly beautiful the act of love could be. And it had taken Judd to teach her.

As if a lizard's claws had scraped her face, Lise was suddenly visited by a paralyzing insight. Why wouldn't Judd be more than competent in bed? He was experienced. He'd had wealthy and sophisticated lovers who traveled in the same world as he. She, Lise, must have seemed impossibly naïve and inept.

What had Angeline said to her once in the back garden in Outremont, on one of her rare visits home after her marriage? "Of course, women throw themselves at him all the time. You can't really blame him for taking what's offered—he's only human, after all.''

At the time, Lise had concluded Angeline was being far too forgiving. Now she felt a blush of shame rush from her chin to her forehead. Last night she, Lise, had offered herself to Judd. He'd had the grace and the forbearance to refuse. But later, in her bed, he'd taken advantage of what she'd so freely made available. And who, indeed, could blame him?

Last night she'd become one in a string of women. She'd cheapened herself in her own eyes, let alone in his. How could she have done that? If she hadn't kissed him so fervently when he'd sat on her bed, if she hadn't fallen into his arms with the ease of a wave curling onto the beach, he'd have left her alone. Kept his promise.

She couldn't stand her own thoughts. Lise jumped out of bed, tossed her nightgown under the pillow and hurried into the bathroom, where she turned on the hot water full force in the shower, and scrubbed herself vigorously with lilac-scented soap to remove every trace of Judd from her skin.

But how was she going to erase him from her memory? Her senses? How to forget the feel of him, the huskiness in his voice when he'd told her how beautiful she was, the laughter and passion and delight he'd brought to her bed?

She would forget him. Eventually. She had to.

Dressing quickly in a bright cotton skirt and peasant blouse that she hadn't worn yet, Lise opened her door and stepped out into the sunlit hallway. If she hesitated, she was lost. Fixing a smile to her lips, she walked into the dining room. "Good morning, Judd...where's Emmy?" she said casually. "Oh good, more papaya. And aren't those fresh croissants?" Her back to him, she poured herself a cup of coffee.

"Emmy's on the beach with Sally and her husband," Judd said. "How did you sleep?"

He sounded so damn sure of himself. So cool, so detached. As if he'd never been within ten feet of her bed. Lise turned around, her face set. "When did you leave my room?"

"Around five. I didn't know what time Emmy might wake."

"We should never have—"

"We did, Lise," he said with menacing softness. "The question is, what do we do now?"

"You take me home. We say goodbye."

"Just like that?"

"What else do you suggest?"

He hesitated fractionally. Then he said in a clipped voice, "A few days ago I mentioned a proposition I had for you."

"You put it into action last night," she said nastily.

"Don't, Lise. Don't cheapen what happened between us."

She put down her fork. "So what did happen, Judd?"

"We made love. Twice." His jaw hardened. "For me it was an unforgettable experience."

"Just like all your other unforgettable experiences."

His eyes flashed as though sunlight had glanced across a knife blade; instinctively she shrank from him. "You're determined to think the worst of me."

"And the worst of myself," she said bitterly.

"Are you saying you regret what happened?"

"Of course!"

"I don't believe you! I was with you, I held you and kissed you and heard you cry out my name—you were being most truly yourself with me. How can you possibly regret that?"

"It was a one-night stand," she cried. "I've never done that before—and I never will again."

Restlessly Judd moved his shoulders. She wasn't telling him anything he didn't already know: that she was a woman of principle. Okay, Judd. Decision time. If you keep your mouth shut, last night stays as a one-night stand, and you don't try to see her again. Ever. Or else you can take a gamble. A huge gamble, because it involves Emmy.

He needed his head read.

Emmy needs Lise.

The three short words replayed themselves in his mind; and Judd knew them for the truth. Not giving himself time to retreat from them, he said flatly, "Why don't you hear me out? About this proposition, I mean." He took a deep breath, feeling his tension level move up another notch. "I'd like you to take a position in my house as Emmy's companion. You'd get her off to school in the mornings, be with her when she comes home, stay with her when I'm away or if she's sick. Your weekends would be free whenever I'm home. But obviously I'd expect you to quit your job at the fire station." He then mentioned a rate of pay that made Lise blink.

She said the first thing that came into her head. "Do you always try to buy people?"

"I'm talking about hiring you. Not buying you."

"And where would I sleep?"

He said with careful restraint, "Once the repairs are finished, you'd have your own suite of rooms off the main wing."

"And in the meantime?"

"We'd all be in the guest wing."

So angry she no longer cared what she said, Lise fumed, "So for an amount of money that, as you must know, is a fortune to me but peanuts to you, you'd be getting a mistress and a nanny all in one? You'll forgive me, I'm sure, if I refuse.''

He stood up, his hands jammed in his pockets. ''You persist in distorting everything I say. You're the one who made a play for me before dinner last night—or are you conveniently forgetting that? And if you didn't enjoy yourself in bed with me, you should quit being a firefighter and become an actress, you'd make a fortune. Listen to reason for a minute. If you lived in my house, you and Emmy could get to know each other better. You wouldn't be so tired. Nor would you be putting your life at risk every day the way you do now.''

Oh, wouldn't I? she thought crazily. Shows what you know, Judd Harwood.

She could have told him she was desperate to quit her job; had been for weeks. She didn't. ''The answer's no,'' she said in a stony voice.

''I am not hiring you as my mistress, as you so charmingly put it.''

''You're not hiring me for anything!''

''You've got to be the most stubborn and contrary woman on the face of this earth,'' Judd grated. ''You'd be good for Emmy, Lise, I know you would.''

''Emmy doesn't even like me.''

''She would. Given time.''

Lise said furiously, ''I'm not going to be the one who salves your conscience so you can travel to all the trendy resorts and society parties and neglect your own child.''

''Is that another direct quote from my ex-wife? Seems to me both of you conveniently manage to forget that I have a job, which requires a fair bit of travel. And which happens, of course, to have paid for this trip.''

Her lips set mutinously. ''So after last night, how much do I owe you?''

He took her by the shoulders, his jaw a tight line. ''A

remark like that is what cheapens you. Not anything you did in bed with me last night, Lise.''

He was right. Of course. Her body slumping in his hold, Lise said with the kind of honesty that only desperation brings, ''Judd, I was a fool to come here. And even more of a fool to wear that dress last night. I'm sorry I made a play for you, I wasn't thinking with anything other than my hormones. The best thing we can do is go our separate ways tomorrow and forget that last night ever happened. Please.''

''Hormones,'' he repeated in an unreadable voice.

''Well, of course. What else could it be? We don't even like each other—we're certainly not in love with each other. So we can't possibly jeopardize Emmy's peace of mind, her security, for something that's no more than lust.'' Then, from the corner of her eye, Lise caught movement. With patent relief she added, ''Thank goodness— here comes Emmy with Sally.''

For a moment Judd's fingers increased their pressure; her head jerked up. ''We're not through with each other— no matter what you say.''

Of their own volition, Lise's eyes fell to his mouth, and instantly she was tortured by memories of how Judd had kissed her last night with such passion and inventiveness. Don't go there, she thought frantically. Not now. ''There are some people you can't control, Judd. And I'm one of them.'' She pulled free of him. ''I'm going to pack. See you later.''

He made no move to stop her; his whole face had closed against her. Lise hurried down the hall and into her bedroom, shutting the door with careful restraint. Then she stared dry-eyed at the room in which she'd found such bliss. The wide bed with its exquisite painting of a blue heron over the headboard. The collection of jade carvings on the recessed shelf against the far wall. A serenely beautiful room she was deliberately leaving, to go back to her real life.

Moving like a robot, she began folding the garments in the closet into her two suitcases, separating those Judd had bought her from the rest. Her brain, belatedly, had begun to work. Why had Judd invited her to become Emmy's companion? He loved Emmy. Why would he risk his beloved daughter growing fond of a woman who was nothing but an employee?

Maybe this time Angeline was right: that Judd always treated people like chessmen on a board, disposable objects to be moved according to his own design and for his own ends. So that he won, Lise thought unhappily. Because winning was the name of his game.

His reasons didn't matter. She'd said no and she'd meant it. Nothing could be more impossible than for her to live in the same house with Judd, no matter how big a house or how often he was away. She couldn't bear to do that. It would destroy her.

Ten hours later the limo drew up outside Lise's apartment block. A messy mixture of snow and ice pellets was falling from a gray sky. The snowbanks edging the streets were dirty, while the pedestrians looked hunched and grumpy. Lise said in a voice that sounded totally artificial, "Emmy, it was lovely being with you. I hope it won't be too hard going back to school. Judd, I—"

"I'll walk you to the door."

"There's no need for—"

The look he gave her would have stopped a fire truck in its tracks. Lise got out of the limo and as he reached in the trunk for the cases, said sharply, "I only want my own."

"Do you have to argue about everything? You're keeping the clothes I bought you and that's the end of it."

The raw cold seemed to have penetrated her very bones. Shivering, Lise said, "This is the end of it, you're right," and prayed he hadn't heard the pain underlying her words. She tramped through the snow to the front door and held it open for him. Then she said, "I can carry the cases, Judd."

He put them down on the floor. His eyes were an impenetrable gray. As cold as the sky, she thought, and said clumsily, "Your villa, the pool, the rain forest—it was all so beautiful...thank you."

As if the words were forced from him, he said, "When you go back to work, for God's sake don't go taking risks."

"I saved Emmy by taking risks."

A muscle twitched in his jaw. "If you change your mind about the job I offered you, call me. Goodbye, Lise."

"Goodbye," she whispered, and watched him walk away from her, out the door, across the sidewalk and into the limo. Which smoothly accelerated into the traffic.

He was gone. He hadn't kissed her, and he'd made no mention of another meeting. He'd gotten the message. Finally.

She took the elevator to her floor. Her apartment looked cramped and untidy. Lise turned up the heat and started to unpack, her own suitcase first, then the one Judd had given her. But when she came to the jade-green dress, her hands stilled. For the space of a few glorious hours, she'd become the kind of woman who could wear such vividly hued and provocatively designed silk. She'd discovered that woman in Judd's arms, clasped to his naked body. But now she had to go back to being herself. Blue jeans. A firefighter's rubber boots.

If Judd hadn't bought that dress, she wouldn't have gone to Dominica. She wouldn't now be paralyzed by a pain that served only to remind her of those dreadful days after her parents died in the fire, when she'd lost everything known and familiar and taken for granted.

If she hadn't gone away with Judd, she'd still have known who she was.

March merged into April. Winter clung to the city, burying the crocuses and early daffodils in layers of snow and freezing rain. Highway accidents abounded; a rash of false fire alarms had every firefighter in the city on edge. Not that Lise wasn't on edge to start with.

The first week she was home she scarcely slept, and when she did, her dreams were haunted by images of Judd. Erotic images, that woke her to an empty bed and a body aching with need. Terrifying images, where he was trapped in a burning jet and she couldn't rescue him. From these she woke drenched in sweat, her heart racing in her breast.

How could he, in so short a time, have affected her so strongly? More pragmatically, how was she to endure the long night hours alone in her apartment? Her only choice seemed to be turning off her body altogether. Driving herself so hard at work that she was tired enough to sleep when she got home.

Forgetting that she had a body. Let alone any sexuality.

The second week was a nightmare. Three people died in a suspected arson. Dave broke his arm in a warehouse fire; Stephan inhaled smoke and ended up in intensive care.

Lise's last shift that week was on Thursday. She got off at six, changed into street clothes and, instead of going home, hurried down the street to the nearest pub. She needed warmth and people and noise. She needed a glass of red wine along with a hot meat pie and French fries smothered in gravy. Too bad about cholesterol. Simple comfort was more important.

She was going to quit her job. The decision had, somehow, coalesced this week. So she needed to strategize how best to do it, and also how to pay for the vet's assistant course she was almost sure would be her next move.

Lise found a table in a secluded corner, placed her order and let the first mouthful of wine slide down her throat. Then she uncapped her pen, took out her notebook and began totting up her finances, frowning prodigiously. If only she hadn't blown so much money on her trip to Paris and Provence last summer; it had made a huge dent in her savings. Money she could now have used.

"May I join you?"

Lise would have known that voice anywhere. As her heart gave a treacherous leap of mingled panic and joy, she looked up. "Hello, Judd."

He looked impossibly handsome in dark cords, a leather bomber jacket and a deep blue sweater, his black hair disarrayed by the wind. He flung his jacket over the back of the chair and sat down; the waitress, Lise noticed sardonically, came to their table immediately. After Judd had ordered a beer with fish and chips, he leaned forward, his eyes running over her face. "You look god-awful," he said succinctly.

"How did you know I'd be here?"

"I followed you from work."

"Really?" she snapped. "And why did you do that?"

"Figured it was time I tried buying you again," he said with a feral grin.

She took a big gulp of wine. "I don't come cheap."

"You said a mouthful there," Judd said acerbically.

"You're a born manipulator."

"I just work on the facts."

"You work on other people's weaknesses."

Judd raised his brows. "You're admitting to having some?"

Oh, yes, Lise thought, I have weaknesses: one of them's

sitting right across from me. And dammit all, for the first time in two weeks, I feel alive.

The waitress deposited Judd's beer in front of him. He raised his glass. *"Salut."*

She said levelly, "Are you reoffering me the job as Emmy's companion?"

"At double the salary," he remarked.

Lise played with her glass, watching light dance fiery-red in the swirling wine. How clever of Judd to wait until her resistance was at its lowest ebb, when she was over-whelmed by the horrifying images of the last few shifts. Her resources drained, her tiredness bone-deep.

She had to leave her job, before she cracked under the strain. Or—perhaps worse—withdrew all her humanity and stopped caring.

Her gaze shifted to her notebook, the numbers mocking her with their inadequacy. If she went to work for Judd, in four months she could save enough for the vet's assistant course. And she could hand in her notice at the fire station; she was only required to give two weeks. She'd more than proved she could hold her own in a male-dominated world; she'd be finished with a job that was pushing her to the limits of her endurance.

Feeling her heart racket around in her rib cage, she said slowly, "I won't commit to any longer than four months."

Had she been watching Judd, she would have seen triumph flare in his eyes, and as quickly be extinguished. He leaned forward. "Why only four months?"

"Because that's long enough to save the money I need for a course I want to take."

"What kind of course?" Judd rapped. After she'd briefly described it, he added, "You've got this all thought out."

"I've wanted to quit the station for at least six months."

"You never told me that."

"No, Judd, I never told you that."

"What else aren't you telling me, Lise?"

"That's for you to find out," she said, and smiled at the waitress. The meat pie smelled delicious; for the first time in days she had an appetite. She could leave her job. Start afresh. She gave Judd a brilliant smile and picked up her fork.

He said evenly, "I'm not sure I'll ever understand you."

"You're hiring me as Emmy's companion, not yours. So you don't have to."

"When can you start?"

"In a couple of weeks."

"What about your apartment?"

"At the salary you're paying me, I can afford to keep it—I'll need it in four months' time."

"And what if Emmy has gotten fond of you by then?"

The smile died from Lise's lips. "You should have thought of that before you offered me the job." She hesitated. "Let's be frank here, Judd. We're using each other—you won't have to worry about Emmy being lonely when you're away, and I'll save the better part of twelve thousand dollars. This arrangement, in other words, is to our mutual advantage. And I'll be sure to tell Emmy right from the start that it's only temporary."

"You've covered all the angles but one."

She knew immediately what he meant. As color mounted in her cheeks, she announced, "There'll be no repeat of what happened in Dominica—you'll have to agree to that before I'll even think of moving in."

"You'd have to agree to it, too, Lise. You were, after all, the instigator."

"I wish I'd never seen that dress!"

"Eat your French fries," Judd said, "you've lost weight."

"Whereas you look in the pink of health."

"I knew I was going to see you again. I just wasn't sure when," he said blandly. "Were you pining for me, Lise?"

"Get off my case."

He laughed. "Your hair's just as red and your temper hasn't suffered. What kind of dreams have *you* been having?"

Lise choked on a chip, hastily gulped some wine and strove for a semblance of dignity. "Nightmares," she said, "with you as the main character."

He suddenly sobered. "Emmy had one last night. Which is yet one more reason I followed you here."

"I don't think I'm the person to help her with those."

"I believe you are," he said with finality, and with equal finality changed the subject. "Do you come here often?" She nodded. "Alone?"

"Not always."

"How's Dave?" Judd asked, his eyes watchful on her face.

She shivered. "He broke his arm on Monday in that warehouse fire...he could very easily have been killed."

Judd said with sudden violence, "Will you please take care of yourself the next two weeks?"

She looked at him in puzzlement. "You sound very vehement."

"It's an entirely accurate reflection of how I feel," Judd said, squeezing lemon on his fish with vicious strength.

"You're not in *love* with me, Judd?"

"Let me tell you something. I fell in love with Angeline when I was twenty-three—you were there, you must have seen how I felt about her. I worshiped the ground she walked on. But our marriage didn't work out. The long-term effect was to immunize me against ever falling in love again. Been there, done that, got the T-shirt. Once was enough, in other words."

"Do you still love her?" Lise blurted.

"What would be the point?"

Which, thought Lise, wasn't really an answer at all. And who could blame him if he did? At the height of her modeling career, Angeline had been voted one of the ten most beautiful women in the world.

"To get back to the dangers of your job," Judd said tautly. "I don't have to be in love to hate the thought of you falling six stories through a burning building."

Her emotions in a turmoil—because hadn't Judd as much as admitted he was still in love with his ex-wife, a woman he had treated very badly?—Lise said, "I'm always careful. I don't want to end up a statistic in the annual report."

"When's your last shift?"

She pulled her daybook out of her backpack, flipping through the pages. "Two weeks from today. I get off at eight."

"I'll pick you up first thing Friday morning. That'll give you time to get settled before Emmy's off school for the weekend."

Two weeks from tomorrow. "You know something?" Lise said faintly. "I'm certifiably insane to have agreed to this. You and I are adults, presumably we can look after ourselves. But Emmy—I don't want to hurt Emmy." She leaned forward, her face passionate with sincerity. "Get someone else to look after her, Judd. Someone who'll stay and give her the security she needs. Not me."

In a voice like steel, Judd said, "It's too late to back out—you've agreed to come."

Her chips were cold and soggy, and the congealed gravy turned her stomach. Lise pushed her plate away. There was one more question she should have asked. What if she herself grew fond of Emmy? What then?

But she hadn't thought to ask it, and it was too late now.

She'd let a man's implacable will move her around the board as if she had no will of her own. A pawn to his king.

Checkmate, indeed.

CHAPTER EIGHT

"FINISHED with your dinner, ma'am?"

The waitress was standing by their table. "Yes, thanks," Lise stumbled. "No dessert, just coffee."

"Same here," Judd said. As the young woman hurried off, he added harshly, "You look like your best friend just died."

"I'm frightened," she whispered. "And I don't scare easy."

Judd's fingers tightened round his knife. Then he put it down, reached over and covered her hand with his own, saying forcefully, "Lise, it'll be all right. You'll see."

His palm was warm, his fingers lean and strong. As heat raced along Lise's arm into her body, desire pounced on her, predator to prey; desire was always lying in wait for her when she was anywhere in Judd's vicinity. "I can't live in your house!" she cried. "I just can't—we're mad to even consider it."

"Cream and sugar, ma'am?"

Her cup of coffee had been plunked in front of her, brown liquid slopping into the saucer. "Yes," said Lise. "Please."

The waitress then presented Judd with the bill. "You two have a nice evening," she said.

Waiting until she was out of earshot, Judd said coldly, "You hate the ground I walk on, don't you?"

Did she? Was it that simple? "It doesn't matter how I feel about you," Lise responded with equal coldness. "Emmy is my only concern for the next four months.

Emmy, not you.'' She added in open challenge, ''Will she be seeing her mother in that four months?''

''Angeline can see her anytime she chooses.''

''That's not an answer.''

''It's all the answer you're getting.''

The coffee tasted like dishwater and Lise was suddenly exhausted. She opened her wallet and threw a bill on the table. ''I'll see you in two weeks.''

''Eight-thirty Friday morning. I've got meetings at ten.''

Rap music battering her eardrums, the fetid air making her dizzy, Lise stood up and pulled on her jacket. ''I may emigrate to Mongolia,'' she announced. ''Do you think the yaks would like my dress?''

''Anything with an ounce of red blood in it would like your dress,'' Judd said. ''I happen to own Air Mongolia—you can let me know what the service is like.''

''The only way I can afford to fly to Mongolia is as a stowaway,'' she said pithily. ''Goodbye, Judd.''

''See you, Lise,'' he said with a grin that both infuriated and entranced her.

She strode out of the pub and into the crisp evening air. Exhausted she might be. Ready to go home she wasn't. Impulsively she decided to visit Marthe and tell her about the new job. It beat going back to the dishes in the sink. Or sitting on the chesterfield, along with a pile of unfolded laundry, thinking about Judd. Pulling on her mitts, Lise set off at a brisk pace down the sidewalk.

She was near the bus stop when a man's voice hailed her. Dave was across the street, waving at her. She dodged through the traffic, disproportionately pleased to see him. ''Hi,'' she said, glancing at his cast. ''How's the arm?''

''I've been shifted to admin for the next month,'' he said. ''You know how I love filling in forms. Got time for a coffee?''

Five minutes later they were seated in the local coffee

bar, which played jazz rather than rap and served drinkable coffee into the bargain. They chatted a few minutes, then Lise said abruptly, "Dave, I don't want you hearing this from someone else—I'm handing in my notice tomorrow."

He put down his mug so sharply that coffee slopped on the table. "You're quitting."

"I'm burned-out. No pun intended."

"You could join me in the office for a while. Simple."

"I can't—I need a change, Dave. A complete change. I'm sick of disasters and tragedies and night shifts. So I'm going to take a course to be a vet's assistant." She took a deep breath. "In the meantime, I've been offered a job as sort of a live-in nanny. That way I can save some money."

"Sort of a nanny?" Dave said quizzically.

"Remember the little girl in the attic, three weeks ago? It's with her."

"The one whose father I met in the hospital." Dave gave her an inimical look. "I didn't know you'd kept in touch with him."

"I knew him years ago—he's my cousin's ex-husband."

"You want to watch out. He looked like the kind of guy who takes what he wants and too bad about the consequences."

"I can look after myself," Lise said; and wondered how true that was.

"He didn't like the way you and I were kidding around."

"Dave, it's a job, that's all. A job." If she said that often enough, would she start to believe it?

"I'll miss you," Dave said. "I just wish—"

Distressed, Lise said, "I'm so sorry, Dave—but I know I'm not the one for you. Once I'm not around, maybe you'll find someone else, you're such a good man and—"

"So why aren't you interested?"

Because a man with hair black as the night and eyes gray-blue as the sea has taught me about passion...she couldn't possibly say that. "It's just the way it is," she said helplessly. "I—won't you wish me well? And I'd really like to keep in touch."

He said soberly, "Take care of yourself, that's all."

He was the second man to tell her that this evening. A few minutes later she said goodbye to him on the sidewalk and ran for her bus. She was burning bridges right and left, she realized with a frisson along her spine. She'd tell her aunt tonight, and tomorrow she'd hand in her notice. It really would be too late then to change her mind.

Her aunt was home, and offered the usual cool cheek to be kissed. Lise was given a very small glass of sherry. After they'd discussed the weather, Lise said with rather overdone nonchalance, "Oh, by the way, *Tante,* I'm leaving my job at the fire station in a couple of weeks. As an interim position, I'm going to be a companion for your granddaughter, Emmy. I thought you might be pleased to hear that."

"You mean that man hired you?"

"Emmy's father? Yes."

"Lise, don't be ridiculous—you must stay away from him! He'll ruin your life the way he did Angeline's."

"I'm not planning on marrying him, *Tante.*"

"He doesn't marry his women anymore," Marthe said bitterly. "Just discards them when he's done."

Lise said with assumed calm, "Then I'll be a good influence for Emmy."

"You're not listening to me! Let me show you something," Marthe said, spots of color in her withered cheeks. She fumbled among the magazines on an antique cherrywood table, pulling out a plastic folder and passing it to Lise. "This will change your mind."

Nervousness fluttering in her chest, Lise opened the folder. Her aunt had cut photos from society magazines and glued them into a makeshift scrapbook; each picture had Judd in it. Judd with a woman, always a beautiful woman in designer clothes, elegant and aristocratic. Almost never the same woman, Lise noticed with a sinking heart. Quickly she flipped through the pages. The pictures were undated, nor were their sources given. But why should that matter? The message was clear. Judd got around. Judd changed women as easily as he changed his clothes. What else did she need to know?

The last photo was of a striking brunette in a Valentino gown at the opening of the opera in Milan; Judd was smiling down at her, his tuxedo emphasizing his arrogant masculinity. So this is what jealousy is like, Lise thought miserably. A knife being twisted in her heart.

Marthe said sharply, "You're in love with him."

Lise's head jerked up. "I'm not!"

"He won't pay someone like you any attention. You're not beautiful like Angeline, and you don't have money. Nothing to recommend you."

It was the message of Lise's childhood; yet it still had the power to wound. However—and this Marthe must never know—Judd had paid attention to her. For one night on a tropical island, he'd made love to her as if she were the only woman in the world.

She wasn't. And how that hurt.

Drawing on all her fortitude, Lise closed the folder and replaced it on the table. "As you say, I'll be quite safe— I'm not his type at all. And I do believe I'll be good for Emmy." Rather proud of herself, she added with a trace of mischief, "And aren't you glad I won't be wearing firefighter's boots anymore?"

Marthe said fractiously, "You make a joke out of everything. When I talk to Angeline, I'll tell her how stupidly you're behaving.''

"How is Angeline?''

"She's very unhappy. Her husband, so she believes, is having an affair…I want her to come home, but she insists her place is with him.'' Marthe sighed. "She's very loyal.''

Lise had had enough. "I must go, *Tante*. I'll let you know how I get on with Emmy. Perhaps I can bring her for a visit one day.''

"He won't let you,'' Marthe said venomously. "He's never forgiven me for being Angeline's mother. He's evil, Lise. Evil through and through.''

Evil? The man who had made love to her with such passion and generosity? Every cell in Lise's body repudiated such a judgment. Quickly she kissed her aunt goodbye and escaped from the overstuffed room. Her heart sore, she started walking home, the images of Judd and all his elegant companions dancing in front of her eyes. Did he bring women like that home to his big stone house? How would she bear it?

But as Lise marched along, swinging her arms to keep warm, a small voice of reason asserted itself. Her aunt had never been known for kindness; and had doted on Angeline with obsessive single-mindedness for as long as Lise could remember. To make a scrapbook like that, to call Judd evil—surely those weren't the acts of a rational woman.

What was the truth about Judd and Angeline's marriage? About Emmy's custody? Would she ever find out?

Two weeks later, at eight o'clock on Thursday night, Lise started to pack for her move to Judd's. Today had been her final day at the fire station; last Saturday the crew had taken her out for dinner, and she had been touched to realize how deeply she'd carved her niche in that over-whelmingly masculine world.

She'd neither seen nor heard from Judd in the interim. He'd be picking her up in the morning to take her to his home for the next four months. Four months. It sounded like forever. But she'd applied for the veterinary course, and the interviews had gone well; so that was something to look forward to.

If she were honest, she was dreading the next four months.

Snow was whirling outside the window in eddies as pale as ghosts. Maybe the blizzard would go on all weekend, she thought hopefully, and she could stay right where she was. She folded two shirts and placed them in her case, adding jeans and a couple of turtlenecks. Rummaging in the bathroom cabinet, she added shampoo and conditioner. Then she knocked a box off the shelf: her tampons. She'd need those, she thought casually, and started stuffing them in a corner of her case.

Her hands suddenly stilled. Ice encased her heart as her brain frantically started making calculations. How long since she'd taken this box out of the cabinet? Since she'd had a period? She was overdue. Two weeks overdue.

She counted backward on her fingers. Sixteen days over-due.

She was never late. She could set a calendar by her cycle, she was so regular.

No. Oh God, no. She couldn't be pregnant. She couldn't be.

She and Judd had used no protection. When he'd burst into her room the night the lizard had run across her face, he'd been wearing nothing but his briefs. And it hadn't exactly been a planned seduction. Anything but.

She was pregnant.

With a whimper of distress, Lise buried her face in her

hands, her shoulders bowed. Could it be true? Was she really pregnant? Or had all the stresses of the past few weeks conspired to knock her off schedule? Hadn't she, purposely, tried to shut her body down ever since she'd left Dominica, in an effort to cope with her desperate longing for Judd?

There was a drugstore five blocks away where she could get a pregnancy test. But she'd already heard on the radio that most businesses had closed early due to the storm. Nor would she have time in the morning before Judd picked her up.

How was she going to face him with this nightmare hanging over her head?

She wasn't pregnant. Of course she wasn't. For once in her life her timing was off. And with good reason. Judd's lovemaking had turned her into a different woman, one she'd never known existed. Why wouldn't this be reflected in her body's rhythms?

But the ice had spread from her heart to the rest of her body, all the way to her fingertips. She'd taken her pleasure. And now she was paying for it.

If she truly were pregnant, she couldn't possibly stay at Judd's for four months: he'd find out. How could she have been so reckless as to make love with him, and so stupid to ignore something as rudimentary as birth control?

Because she'd fallen in love with him? All over again as an adult?

Oh, no, Lise thought grimly, I'm not going that route. There's no way I'd fall in love with a man I neither like nor respect. Not an option.

I'm not thirteen. I'm twenty-eight.

Automatically she shoved a pile of socks and underwear into her suitcase; and added the box of tampons. Because she'd be needing them. Of course she would. In fact, now that she'd realized the problem, she wouldn't be surprised if she got back on track overnight.

Somewhat cheered by this conclusion, Lise folded some skirts, trousers and a couple of dresses. Then she took down the photo of her parents from the bookshelves, rubbing the dust from the gold frame. Her mother's thin, intelligent face, her father's infectious grin: she bit her lip, knowing that at some deep level she still missed them. They'd been wrenched from her so traumatically and so finally amidst the smoke and flames that dreadful February night...and hadn't she, the last ten years, been making reparation over and over again by plunging herself into that same world of fire and tragedy?

Involuntarily her hands gripped the picture frame more tightly. If she were pregnant, she was carrying their grandchild. Extending her parents' bloodline into the future. Briefly, warmth curled soft arms around her, enclosing her in a joy as tender as it was fragile. She must take care of herself. For her unborn child's sake.

But then Lise's mind made the next leap. She was also bearing Judd Harwood's child. Fruit of his body, son or daughter of his name. Just as much his as Emmy was.

He'd want the child for himself—wouldn't he? He hadn't allowed Angeline custody of Emmy. Why would he allow her, Lise, to keep this second child?

One more pawn on his chessboard.

She wouldn't let him take her child. She couldn't.

Lise suddenly became aware she'd bitten her lip until it bled. What was she thinking of? She didn't even know for sure she was pregnant, and she was already worrying herself sick over what Judd might do. Tomorrow morning she'd ask him to stop by the drugstore on their way to his house. She had to know, one way or the other.

Quickly Lise finished packing. Then she spent three hours wielding a dustcloth and the vacuum cleaner, until the apartment had never looked better and she felt tired enough to sleep.

She did sleep. But when she got up to the beep of the alarm the next morning, she soon realized that she was now seventeen days late. No miracles in the night. Only a stretching of her nerves to the breaking point.

She dressed in a denim skirt with a purple silk shirt she'd bought on sale. After pulling her hair back with a leather barrette, Lise made up her face with care, using more blusher than usual, and a bright lipstick. Lastly she pulled on her tall boots and hunter-green wool coat, also bought on sale. Pirouetting in front of the mirror, she decided she looked just fine. Businesslike. Carefree. In control.

What she didn't see was the deep uncertainty in her green eyes, or the tension along her jawline. But when she opened the door to Judd five minutes later, his gaze flew to her face. "You look like you're going to your own funeral," he rapped.

His slate-gray eyes seemed to see right through her, stripping her of everything but confusion and terror. Deliberately she counterattacked. "You don't look so good yourself."

"Don't I? That's because I wasn't taking it for granted you'd be here. You did mention Mongolia."

"Is winning that important to you?"

"I wonder if you'll ever quit thinking the worst of me?"

"I decided in Dominica that you were a good father," Lise blurted, then paled involuntarily. What if she were to make him a father for the second time? What then?

"Lise, what the hell's the matter?"

He was gripping her by the shoulders of her coat, his face only inches from hers; she wanted to kiss him so badly that she could feel the warm, sure pressure of his lips against her own. Pulling back, Lise said jaggedly,

"I've committed myself to the next four months in your house—what else could be the matter?"

His expletive made her wince. "Let's go," he said harshly. "The streets are a mess, and I don't want to be late for my meeting. Is this all you're bringing?"

He picked up the two larger cases, while Lise took her overnight bag. With a feeling of fatality, she locked the door of her apartment behind her, and went down in the elevator with Judd. He was driving a sleek navy-blue Cherokee with leather upholstery; he piled the cases in the back, and Lise climbed in. As they pulled away from the curb, she said, "I couldn't get to the drugstore last night. Would you mind stopping at the nearest one—it'll only take me a minute."

He nodded curtly. She looked out the window, trying to think of something to say and failing miserably. Judd parked in the lot to one side of the mall and pocketed his keys, reaching for the handle on his door. Lise faltered, "There's no reason for you to come—I won't be long."

"Emmy needs a new toothbrush."

"I'll pick one up for her."

He gave her a sharp look. "You planning on running away?"

"I've had two weeks to do that."

"Then let's go," he ordered. "My time's limited."

Lise trailed into the drugstore, bought an assortment of things she didn't need, and paid for them. She didn't even look in the relevant section; what was the use? On Monday, as soon as Emmy was in school, she'd get a bus downtown. Which meant she had to live with suspense for three more days.

It seemed like a life sentence.

She sat in silence as they drove to Judd's house, which, as before, took her breath away with its elegant proportions, the stone a soft gray against the snow, smoke drifting from one of the many chimneys. As he pushed open the oak front door, Judd said, "The repairs should be finished in the next two to three weeks, and then you can move into your own suite of rooms."

However, Lise's bedroom and private bathroom in the guest wing were spacious and attractive; they were also next door to Emmy's room, on the far side of which Judd was sleeping. Too close, thought Lise, and heard him say, "The staff all know you're here and will help out in any way they can. Emmy's home for lunch and then again at three. I expect to be out all day and most of the evening."

So for today, at least, she didn't have to endure Judd's company. He rasped, "Do you have to look so relieved?"

"I don't know why you're angry," she cried. "You've got what you wanted—I'm here to look after Emmy and you can stay out all night if that's what turns you on."

"I'll tell you what turns me on," Judd said, and planted a kiss full on her mouth. A brief kiss, fired by a mixture of anger and desire that made the blood rocket through Lise's veins. Hunger flowered in its wake; she swayed toward him, and in a distant part of her brain knew she would do it all over again: fall into his arms and into his bed without a thought for the consequences.

What kind of woman did that make her?

A very foolish woman.

"Don't ever deny that you want me, Lise. It's written all over you."

His voice was hard, without a trace of emotion; and suddenly she knew what was wrong. "But you don't want me anymore—not really," she said in a voice she scarcely recognized as her own. "What's free for the taking, you despise—you told me that once."

"I also told you I wasn't bringing you here as a resident mistress. And I meant it."

She cried, "Then why am I here?"

"Money. Isn't that what you said? Twelve thousand dollars."

He was right. She said tonelessly, "You'll be late for your meeting."

"Lise, I—" He broke off. "You'll do just fine. Emmy may take a while to come around, but I know she will sooner or later. Just make yourself at home."

He turned on his heel and was gone. Her knees feeling like wet cardboard, Lise sat down hard on the bed. If Judd didn't want her, why had he kissed her? Simply to assert his mastery? And if he did want her, then why was he so insistent that she wasn't here as his mistress?

None of it made any sense.

Eventually she got up and started to unpack, and gradually grew calmer. Her feet sank into the Chinese carpet that overlaid the wall-to-wall cream pile. The furniture was of waxed pine, the Roman shades and bedspread a soothing pattern of pinks and greens, which was reiterated in two big vases of freshly cut, pink-streaked peonies. Her bathroom was the ultimate in luxury with its gold fittings and deep Jacuzzi.

When she went downstairs, Lise met Maryann the housekeeper again, along with the maids and the groundskeeper. Friendly without being obsequious, they all contrived to make her feel very welcome. Then Emmy arrived home for lunch. The little girl left her snowsuit and boots in the back porch, looking up at Lise through her long dark lashes. "Dad said you're going to live here for four months."

"That's right. Then I'm taking a course so I can help vets with sick dogs and cats," Lise said matter-of-factly.

"I want a dog. But Dad says I'm not quite big enough yet."

"What kind of dog?"

The subject of dogs, cats and horses saw them through

lunch, which they ate in a delightful alcove off the kitchen, overlooking an enclosed orchard. Again the child baffled Lise with her combination of good manners and reserve. Surely it was self-protective. But why?

After school, the two of them played in the snow, Lise helping Emmy build a rotund snowman with a carrot nose and eyes made out of rocks. Emmy had color in her cheeks when they went in, and ate her supper with gusto. Lise helped her in the bath, then read to her from an assortment of books. As Emmy's eyes drooped shut, Lise said softly, "Sleep well, Emmy. I'm just next door if you need me."

"When will Dad be home?"

"Later this evening, he said."

"G'night," Emmy murmured, cuddling her cheek into Plush's body in a way that made Lise want to cry. Blinking, she turned off the light and left Emmy alone, going to her own room and turning on the bathwater. There was a very real risk that she could grow more than fond of Emmy. How to guard against that, she had no idea. She did know something, though. She was going to stay in her own rooms for the rest of the evening, and not risk seeing Judd again.

She was still seventeen days late.

CHAPTER NINE

THE next morning when Lise went downstairs for breakfast, Emmy and Judd were already seated in the alcove, Judd drinking coffee, Emmy devouring oatmeal. Judd was dressed in an immaculate business suit with a figured silk tie. He glanced up as Lise came into the room. "Good morning," he said with crushing formality. "I was just telling Emmy there's been a mix-up in Singapore and I've got to go there right away. I should be back by midweek."

Masking a surge of relief that made her feel light-headed, Lise tried to look as cool and collected as he. She could go to the drugstore Monday when Emmy was in school, and she'd have a couple of days to contemplate the results before she had to face Judd again. "I hope it's not a real emergency," she said.

"Nothing that can't be fixed," he answered dismissively. "By the way, a new Walt Disney movie opened last week, Emmy was wondering if you'd take her."

Lise smiled at the little girl with real warmth. "Of course, I'd love to."

Judd took a sheaf of bills from his wallet. "Here's an advance on your first paycheck," he said coldly. "And this is expense money for things like movies. I don't expect any accounting of it."

She was his employee, that was the message. One among many, Lise thought with painful accuracy, and took the money, stuffing it into her pocket. "Thank you," she said stiffly.

"I'll let Maryann know when I'll be back. I always call

Emmy just before her bedtime when I'm away, so if you could make sure she's available for that."

"Of course." Helping herself from the bowl of fruit salad on the side table, Lise clamped down on her temper: she might hate taking orders from Judd, but she had accepted the job, after all. And wasn't this one more piece of evidence that Judd was a good father?

"We get our report cards on Tuesday," Emmy said. "I'm pretty sure I got all *A*'s."

"We might have to go to McDonald's to celebrate," Judd said with a grin that didn't include Lise.

Lise sliced a flaky croissant in two and slathered it with homemade apricot jam, endeavoring to look on the bright side. She didn't have a trace of morning sickness and her appetite was great; so maybe, just maybe, she wasn't pregnant. Monday. She'd know Monday. Not much longer to wait.

Once Judd had left, Lise purposely kept Emmy busy; and was rewarded with the first sense that the barrier between Emmy and her might be lowering. Emmy wanted to talk about the movie afterward, something Lise always liked to do; when Judd phoned, at seven-thirty on the nose, Lise heard Emmy mention her own name several times.

Judd didn't ask to speak to her. For which, Lise told herself fiercely, she was glad. What did she have to say to him? That in thirty-six hours she'd know if she were pregnant by him?

Actually it was closer to thirty-eight hours. And the pregnancy test came up positive. Lise sat down hard on the bed in her own apartment. She was carrying Judd's child. She was going to be a mother. Amidst a turmoil of emotion she was aware of a shaft of pure, unquenchable joy.

She clutched it to her. Later she'd worry about the enormous difficulties of her situation: the unforeseeable and undeniable consequences of an unplanned, ill-judged pregnancy. But for now she was happy. Quickly she picked up the phone and made an appointment with her family doctor for the following week. Then she drove back to Judd's. Of all the complications that surrounded her like a thicket of thorns, only one thing was clear. She wasn't going to tell him. Not yet.

Not ever?

On Wednesday night, Lise went to bed early. Judd was expected home some time that night; she wasn't yet ready to face him. The happiness that had enfolded her in the apartment on Monday had gone underground, leaving her racked by foreboding and nameless fears. Judd saw too much. He was far too intelligent to deceive for long. What was she going to *do*?

The changes in her body would take place inevitably and according to their own schedule: nothing she could do about that. The only plan she'd formulated was to stay with Emmy for two months rather than four, save every penny she could, and then move somewhere like Halifax, where she could live more cheaply and take the same veterinary course. Already she'd handed in her notice for her apartment; she couldn't afford to keep it.

Needing comfort, she put on her oldest flannelette nightgown and made herself some hot chocolate before bed. She fell asleep around eleven, a restless sleep in which images of disaster flickered in and out of her mind. When she found herself sitting bolt upright, her heart racing, she thought it was her own dream that had woken her. Then she heard a thin cry of distress from the room next to hers. She was out of bed and into Emmy's room in a flash, gathering the little girl in her arms. "It's all right, Emmy, I'm here," she said. "You're safe, I won't let anything happen to you."

Clutching Lise in her thin arms, Emmy burst into tears. Lise rocked her back and forth, murmuring words of comfort. "Do you want to tell me about it?"

Emmy spilled out a confused story about a huge bonfire and dancers with masks who kept pushing her nearer and nearer the flames. Her heart aching, Lise did her best to defuse the dream's terror; and was rewarded when Emmy snuffled, "I'm glad you're here. Sometimes I m-miss having a mother."

"I'm glad I'm here, too," Lise said; and felt guilt flood her that she would be leaving even sooner than Emmy was expecting. Emmy needed stability; which was just what Lise couldn't give her.

A few moments later, Emmy's body sagged in Lise's arms; she'd fallen asleep. Very carefully Lise lowered her to the bed, tucking the covers around her and making sure Plush was snuggled close. The little girl's fall of dark hair on the pillow, the soft puffs of her breathing, filled Lise with the same tenderness she'd felt earlier toward her unborn child.

If she grew to love Emmy, she'd be in even deeper trouble.

She padded toward the door, wrapped in her own thoughts, and walked right into the man who was standing half-hidden by the door. With a tiny shriek of alarm, she pushed against his chest with her palms. "Judd—you scared me!"

He pulled her away from Emmy's doorway until they were out of earshot. Then he said roughly, "Did she have another nightmare?"

His arms were still around her; he was wearing trousers and a shirt unbuttoned to the waist. The feel of his skin, warm, hair-roughened, lanced Lise with an agony of desire. Taking refuge in anger, she said, "Emmy still misses her mother."

"I heard that."

The one question whose answer she couldn't understand burst from Lise's lips. "How *could* you have denied Angeline custody?"

He said in a voice as cutting as a honed blade, "Let's get something straight, once and for all. I'm sick to death of being the villain in this divorce. Angeline's second husband, who can trace his ancestors back to the fourteenth century, didn't want another man's daughter in his fancy château. Especially a man who haled from the worst tenements in Manhattan. So Angeline very prettily decided Emmy would be better off in a familiar environment with me."

"That's not—"

"Angeline had an affair two years before that. In New York. She's not clever enough to hide her tracks, so I found out. She didn't really understand why I was so upset. You need to know something about your cousin—what she wants in the moment, she takes. Like a kid on a hot day stealing a carton of ice cream, not realizing it'll melt and make a big mess before she can eat it all. Angeline's not a bad person. She just doesn't understand that there are consequences to her actions. That people can get hurt in the process."

"But—"

"We patched that one up. More or less. But then along came Henri, rich, aristocratic and available. Angeline doesn't like conflict. So she wrote me a note, left me to do the explaining to Emmy, and took the Concorde to Paris. End of story. I divorced her. It was only later, when I took Emmy to visit Marthe, that I realized that Angeline, no doubt with the best of intentions, was delicately suggesting to all and sundry that I'd been less than ethical in my dealings with her." He moved his shoulders restlessly.

"I could have sued her, I suppose, for defamation of character. I chose not to. For Emmy's sake."

His voice had the undeniable ring of truth. But hadn't Angeline's also had that same ring, in those scattered conversations over the years? Although now that Lise looked back, Angeline had never said outright that Judd had taken custody; it had all been insinuated, more in sorrow than in anger. So was Judd right? Was Angeline greedy like a child, with a child's lack of empathy for those she wounded?

Had Lise's worship of her cousin blinded her to Angeline's very real faults, while emphasizing her virtues? Lise said crisply, "The last time I saw Marthe, she showed me a scrapbook full of photos of you with different women. Dozens of photos."

"You never give up, do you?" Judd said unpleasantly. "Everywhere I go, women flock around me—dollar signs in their eyes. I'm not saying I haven't had affairs since the divorce, that wouldn't be true. But I've already told you that the whole time Angeline and I were married, I was faithful to her."

Wondering which of all those women he'd had affairs with, knowing she'd hate them on sight, Lise took a steadying breath. "I didn't know you grew up in poverty."

"I'm not ashamed of it. But I don't go around advertising it, either."

"Are your parents still alive?"

He said in a clipped voice, "I never knew my father, he was gone long before I was born. My mother died when I was five. Of undernourishment and overwork."

In deep distress Lise whispered, "But you were younger than Emmy."

"Don't go feeling sorry for me."

She said quietly, "Where did you live after that?"

"Orphanage. Could have been better, could have been

worse. I always knew I'd be out of there as fast as I could, and that I wouldn't be back...I don't know why I'm telling you this, I never talk about it.'' His clasp tightened on her shoulders, and in the semidarkness his eyes were like shards of slate. "Do you believe me, Lise—that I was faithful to Angeline?''

Lise hesitated a fraction too long. He said with ugly emphasis, "You're going to have to choose. You can believe Angeline. Or you can believe me. One or the other. And until you do, I'm going back to that promise I made before we went to Dominica—and this time, don't try changing my mind. Because it won't work.''

"You're arrogant enough to assume I'd want to change your mind.''

"Yeah,'' he drawled, "I am.''

"You know something? I learned a great many swear-words driving in the fire truck the last ten years, not one of which would do justice to the way I feel right now.''

He let go of her and stepped back. "Then maybe you'd better go back to bed.''

She was pregnant by this man? Halifax, here I come, thought Lise, and said sweetly, "I do hope you sleep well.''

"You might want to buy a new nightgown with some of the money I'm paying you.''

Anger and amusement teetered in the balance; despite herself, amusement won. Lise said, "No way—I've had this since I was seventeen.''

He surveyed her from the ruffles at her throat to the rather frayed frill around her ankles. "Very sexy,'' he said.

"I'm attached to it.'' Lise wrinkled her nose charmingly. "Sort of like Emmy and Plush.''

"You look about seventeen in it.''

"No kidding? Then I'd better hang on to it.''

"Unfortunately it's not acting as a deterrent. I still want to kiss you senseless."

"You can't. You promised," Lise said breathlessly.

"Go to bed, Lise. Now. Alone. And that's an order."

It wasn't the moment to remember how she'd writhed in his arms in the velvety darkness of a Caribbean night. Almost tripping over the hem, Lise hurried to her room, fell into bed and pulled the covers over her head. She was in bed and she was definitely alone; although every fiber of her being ached for Judd to be here with her.

For that to happen, she had to choose which one to believe. Judd, the man she'd made love with. Or Angeline, the cousin she'd adored.

On Sunday Judd, Emmy and Lise went tobogganing on the slopes of Mont-Royal, with its panoramic view of sky-scrapers and the sweep of the St. Lawrence River. Lise, without being too obvious about it, took only the safe runs, leaving Emmy and Judd to go over the jumps and capsize several times. Emmy's cheeks were pink from cold and happiness; Judd looked so young and vital that Lise had to avert her eyes. She was trying very hard to repress the knowledge of her pregnancy, afraid that if she didn't, Judd would take one look at her and discern her secret. But the unfeigned pleasure he was taking in his daughter's company hurt something deep inside her. She couldn't seriously be contemplating moving to Halifax and never telling Judd he was the father of two children, rather than one?

When they got back to the house, they headed for the back door with all their wet gear and Emmy started lobbing snowballs indiscriminately at her father and Lise. Lise retaliated, ducked to avoid a big gob of snow flung by Judd, tripped and fell backward into a deep, fluffy snow-bank. Icy crystals trickled across her cheeks and down her neck. Emmy tumbled on top of her, thrusting more snow down her collar.

Laughing so hard she couldn't stop, Lise gurgled, "That's cold—stop, Emmy! I'll read you six stories before you go to bed, I promise—"

Emmy picked up one last mittful of snow and let it fall over Lise's flushed cheeks. "You're really pretty," she said spontaneously. "I'm glad you live with us, I like you a lot."

The laughter died from Lise's face. She said unevenly, "Thanks, Emmy. I like you, too. Very much."

"That's good," Emmy said. "Dad, can we have hot chocolate when we go in?"

"I think that could be arranged," Judd drawled, and pulled Lise to her feet, keeping hold of her hands so that for the space of a few seconds she was standing close to him. "I agree with you, Emmy—Lise is very pretty."

His eyes were lingering on her mouth; she could almost taste the heat of his lips on hers. In a strangled voice, Lise muttered, "There's cold water running down my back and I want three oatmeal cookies with my hot chocolate."

"A woman of immoderate appetites," said Judd, and released her.

"You got it," she said, and scurried for the back porch, the image of his sculpted mouth shivering along her nerves. As she pushed open the door and stepped inside, the heat hit her like a blow. Her vision blurred. The row of coats hanging on hooks swooped and dived like a flock of great birds, while the floor rushed up to meet her. From an immense distance Lise felt someone grab her before she could hit the gray ceramic tiles.

Her limbs were as useless as spaghetti. Blackness shot with all the colors of the rainbow swirled through her brain. Then she was on the floor, her head shoved between her knees. The colors were swallowed by a red haze.

Dimly wondering if she was going to be sick, Lise heard Emmy's frightened whisper, "Dad, is she okay?"

"Sure," Judd said calmly. "It was just the heat, Emmy. You know Maryann, she likes to keep the place as hot as Dominica."

As Emmy gave a weak giggle, Lise raised her head. "S-sorry," she mumbled. "I don't know what came over me."

"Your face is white, just like the snow," Emmy announced.

Little wonder, thought Lise dazedly; she felt drained and utterly exhausted. She never fainted. Never. Then in a spurt of pure terror she realized the cause must be her pregnancy. Of course. She didn't have morning sickness, but she couldn't hope to escape all the symptoms. She said more strongly, pushing against the floor, "I feel better now, I'm sorry I—"

Judd said forcibly, "Don't be in such an all-fired hurry."

His arms were around her shoulders and she could smell, elusively, the masculine scent of his skin, so achingly familiar, so longed for and so out of reach. Her eyes skidded from the concern in his face. She said clumsily, "I'm fine, Judd, it was just the heat and—"

With genuine interest, Emmy said, "Did you used to faint when you went to fires? Because they're really hot."

Lise gaped at her in horror. Emmy had put her finger on it: Why would an ex-firefighter faint because of a little heat? Say something, Lise, she thought. Anything at all. Because you can't risk Judd guessing why you fainted. "We're already wearing all that gear I showed you," she stumbled. "So we're hot to start with."

Judd interposed, "Why don't you go and ask Maryann to rustle up the hot chocolate, Emmy? I'll take Lise into the den."

Emmy pulled off her boots, hung up her snowsuit and ran for the kitchen. Judd knelt in front of Lise and eased her boots from her feet. Snow had melted in his hair; his lashes were very dark against his cheek. Just as, involuntarily, her hand reached out to brush a strand of hair back from his forehead, he looked up. His eyes burned into hers as though he'd stripped her naked; as though every secret she'd ever harbored must be known to him. Then his mouth plummeted to hers, and another kind of heat surged through her body. With a moan of delight, Lise kissed him back, withholding nothing.

For moments that felt like forever to Lise, their lips clung together, his big body crouched over her. From behind them, Emmy said, "That's what people do when they're going to get married. My friend Charlene told me."

Judd's mouth wrenched itself from Lise's. He surged to his feet and for the first time in their acquaintance Lise saw that he was at a loss for words. Emmy added, her heart-shaped face alive with interest, "Is that why Lise came to live here? Because you're going to get married?"

"No!" Judd raked his fingers through his disordered hair. "Of course not. She's here to look after you, Emmy. That's all."

"Then why were you—"

"There are some things you won't understand until you're older," he said repressively. "Did you ask Maryann about the hot chocolate?"

"She thought you might want coffee instead. That's why I came back."

"You go and tell her hot chocolate's fine, Emmy."

Emmy headed for the kitchen, her mouth a mutinous line. Judd said irritably, "She's quite intelligent enough to know she's been given the brush-off. I was a fool to even touch you. It won't happen again. Believe me."

Lise did. Bereft, aroused, furious, frightened...what

other emotions were left for her to feel? She pushed herself to her feet, staggering a little, and faltered, "This evening I'll remind her that I'm only here temporarily."

"You do that."

"I don't understand why you're so angry—you're the one who kissed me!"

"You think I don't know that?" he exploded. "You just have to look at me with those big green eyes and I act with as much common sense as a teenager. And about as much restraint."

"And how you hate it," she whispered.

"That's as good a word as any for the way I feel right now."

"So why don't you fire me before we get into any worse trouble? Emmy already likes me...oh God, Judd, I should never have come here."

"You know what?" he snarled. "I've built up an international fleet of airlines, made a fortune into the bargain, and everything I've ever learned flies out the window when I'm anywhere near you. Explain that to me, will you?"

"Basic chemistry. Your words."

His expletive made her wince. He said flatly, "I'm going to the kitchen before Emmy comes looking for us again. One last thing, Lise—what happened just now, it's not going to happen again. Do you hear me?"

"You're repeating yourself," she retorted, and hauled down the zipper on her parka. "You loathe being out of control, Judd Harwood, that's your problem."

"I also loathe being psychoanalyzed!"

"Especially when it's a mere woman who's gotten to you," she added recklessly, hauling off her toque and shaking out her hair.

Judd took a step closer to her, tipping up her chin with one finger. "There's something you ought to know about

me—I pick up challenges that other men run from. So
don't push me too far.''

Her eyes dropped from the threat in his, as instinctively
she stepped backward. But her voice, she was proud to
notice, sounded quite sure of itself. ''Hadn't you better find
Emmy?''

''Remember what I've just said. For your own sake.''

He strode down the hall toward the kitchen. Although
adrenaline was charging through her veins, Lise's knees
still felt as shaky as a day-old kitten's. For a woman
known to keep her cool in emergencies, she wasn't doing
very well.

But at least Judd wasn't suspicious about her dizziness.

He hated being around her. The last thing he needed to
know was that she was carrying his child.

A couple of days later Lise, Emmy and Judd were eating
lunch together in the solarium. Another symptom of pregnancy seemed to be an overriding lethargy; Lise felt tired
and dull-witted, and was glad to let Emmy carry the bulk
of the conversation. At the end of the meal, Judd said
curtly, ''Once Emmy's gone back to school, Lise, would
you come to my office for a minute?''

''Of course,'' she said coolly.

When she tapped on his door, he got up from his desk,
his expression inscrutable. ''Are you coming down with
the flu? You don't look your best.''

Her lashes flickered. ''I'm fine,'' she replied. ''That
wasn't why you wanted to see me, surely?''

''I'll be out of town from Thursday until the following
Tuesday,'' Judd rapped. ''I've left the details of my trip
in this envelope, you'll only need to open it if I'm de-
layed.''

''You're away a lot,'' Lise said, giving him an unfriendly stare.

"I moved to Montreal with the mistaken idea that it would be nice for Emmy to stay in touch with her grandmother," Judd said tersely. "By the time it became obvious that was a lost cause, Emmy had settled in here and made friends. So I stayed. But the upshot is I have to travel a lot."

"Be honest, Judd. You value money more than people. Business comes first—Angeline used to complain about that."

"Once her career took off, Angeline did photo shoots all over the world," Judd snapped. "Although I'm damned if I know why I'm justifying what I do to you."

"No wonder Emmy gets lonesome."

"She doesn't have to be lonesome now that you're here."

"You're her father. Her ultimate security."

"You're determined to pick a fight, aren't you?" he accused. "I told you to choose between Angeline's version of our marriage and mine. I can see that you've decided to believe my ex-wife. Good for you. Just don't go poisoning Emmy's mind against me, will you?"

Lise's head snapped up. "You think I'd do *that?*"

"How do I know?" Scowling, he added, "Take tomorrow off—I want to tell Emmy my plans and spend some extra time with her."

A day away from Judd sounded like heaven. Because being with him was sheer hell.

Hell? Lise thought in faint dismay. That was a strong word. She really did need a day off. A day away from Judd Harwood, his daughter and his business trips.

Maybe he was going to see a woman. Why else would he leave the details of his trip in a sealed envelope?

She'd start cleaning out her apartment tomorrow, she

thought fiercely. It was a job she was dreading. But it would keep her mind off Judd. And his women.

Or one particular woman. The one he'd be with the next few days. How she detested the thought of him in another woman's arms!

CHAPTER TEN

JUDD left on Thursday, with the briefest of goodbyes to Lise. On Friday afternoon, while Emmy was in school, Lise went to her family doctor and was told that she was indeed pregnant. She took the pamphlets he offered about nutrition and health care, evaded his tactful questions and drove back to Judd's.

Emmy brought three friends home from school, which kept Lise satisfactorily busy. But once Emmy was in bed, Lise went to her room. Too restless to read, she flicked on the TV, watched a sitcom during which she didn't laugh once, and then switched to the news channel. Posturing politicians, terrorist bombings, demonstrations...then a dusty airstrip surrounded by listless trees. One of the two planes involved in a Red Cross relief airlift into the Sudan had crashed; the camera zoomed in to show a group of people standing by the second plane, and suddenly her attention sharpened.

She'd know that man anywhere, the tall, black-haired man dressed in a scruffy khaki shirt and bush pants. Judd. Judd in Africa delivering food and medical supplies to refugees, when he was supposed to be on a business trip. With a woman.

It couldn't be Judd. But it was. The announcer's voice said that there'd been no fatalities, and the next clip began. Lise ran from her room, went to Judd's study and ripped open the white envelope. In it, neatly typed, was his itinerary from Montreal all the way to the Sudan, with a list of phone numbers where he could be contacted at all times.

He wasn't away on business. He wasn't making more

money. He certainly wasn't with one of the elegant women in Marthe's photos. Instead he was working for the Red Cross under circumstances both dangerous and difficult. Remembering how she'd accused him of being mercenary, Lise cringed with shame.

Once again he'd taken her by surprise. And Angeline's assessment of his character was beginning to seem more and more unlikely...ruthless businessmen motivated entirely by greed didn't risk their lives flying aid planes for refugees. Lise suddenly found herself sitting down hard in Judd's leather-backed chair. The other plane had crashed. There was a very real risk in what he was doing.

If something happened to him, she couldn't bear it.

Hunched over, her arms wrapped tightly around her belly, Lise sat very still. Judd was right. She did have to choose between his version of events and Angeline's. She couldn't have it both ways. Against her lifelong loyalty to her beautiful cousin with her casual kindnesses, she had to balance a man who had made love to her with passionate intensity, who adored his small daughter and who was willing to risk his life for the sake of people far less fortunate than he.

Trust, she thought. Which one do I trust?

Surely you learned something about a man when you made love with him? Judd's total attention, his care of her, his eliciting from her of a passion she hadn't known herself capable of—didn't all that add up to a man who gave as well as received? His face had been as naked to her as his body, she thought humbly. He, too, had been shaken by the sheer intensity of their mating. Hadn't he called it unforgettable?

Ever since he'd told her about his background, she'd carried an image in her mind of a little boy with a shock of black hair consigned to an orphanage in one of the world's biggest cities. Bereft of family. Brought up by strangers. That had to have marked him, to have shaped the man he'd become.

Whereas Angeline had grown up with a mother who doted on her, unable to refuse her anything. To Marthe, her daughter's external beauty mirrored equal beauties of soul. But was that true? Indulgence of every wish perhaps wasn't the best thing for a young girl. Neither was uncritical worship. Who could blame Angeline if she'd grown up with a child's greediness for pleasure and love? Marthe had to bear some of the blame for that. Furthermore, how could Angeline have learned about responsibility if Marthe had always shielded her daughter from the consequences of her actions?

These were new thoughts for Lise. Long overdue thoughts, she decided, and got up from the chair. She should go back to her room, just in case Emmy woke.

For a moment she looked around her. The desk was antique walnut, the carpet delicately faded Tibetan wool. Over the desk hung an oil painting of the desert: ochre sand, gray-green sage, a huge bowl of blue sky. Space, she thought. A landscape that challenged. A dangerous landscape. Judd had grown up in a hostile environment, he knew what it was like to fight for his life.

These, too, were new thoughts. Am I falling in love with him? Is that what's happening? Don't, Lise, don't. He doesn't love you. He's sworn he'll never fall in love again.

With anyone. Including you.

As tears shimmered in her eyes, Lise fought them back. She couldn't have Judd now any more than all those years ago. He was out of reach, as impossible to attain as it would be for her to purchase his house on a firefighter's salary. But she was carrying his child, and for that she was passionately grateful. Never mind about the difficulties, the sacrifices that would be called for. She would be the mother of Judd's child. If she couldn't have Judd, that was the next best thing.

Lise went back to bed and fell asleep; and the weekend, despite a constant undertow of worry about Judd's safety, was oddly peaceful and fulfilling. While she was still subject to occasional dizziness, there was color back in her cheeks from all the time she and Emmy were spending outdoors. Deliberately she chose to ignore that the bond was imperceptibly deepening between her and Judd's daughter. There was nothing she could do to prevent it, and both of them were enjoying it.

Judd was due back Tuesday afternoon; on Monday night Lise put on her old nightgown, took a bundle of magazines to bed and switched off her light about eleven. She'd see Judd again tomorrow, she thought, curling up under the covers; and was aware of a confused mingling of panic and happiness. Conjuring up the image of his face, she hugged it to her and eventually drifted into a deep sleep.

Lise lay still under the covers, her eyes wide-open. Was it a noise that had woken her? Or a deep intuition of another person where there should only have been herself and Emmy? Every nerve on edge, she heard the soft fall of footsteps in the hallway. Her heart gave a great lurch. How could an intruder have gotten past the security system? And what should she do?

There was a phone in Judd's room. She'd sneak in there and dial 911. Moving with extreme care, she sat up and eased her legs free of the covers. The digital clock by her bedside said 3:18 a.m.

Lise edged across the thick carpet toward the door, which she always left ajar, the better to hear Emmy. On the way, she picked up the smooth marble carving of a dolphin that stood on the lacquered table; it was reassuringly heavy in her grip. Cautiously she peered around the door.

The hall was empty. She had to pass Emmy's room to get to Judd's. Clutching the statue in her right hand, her heart thrumming in her chest so loudly she was sure the intruder must hear it, she crept along the cool oak flooring. The boards had been laid impeccably; not one of them creaked. Emmy's door, too, was ajar; silent as a ghost, Lise slid past it and glided toward Judd's bedroom.

It was empty. In one swift glance Lise took in the taupe linen that covered the walls, the cream linen on the big bed. Two huge Schefflera plants flanked French doors that led out onto a terrace. The room's single painting was an abstract, a shimmer of greens and blues. Swiftly she reached for the phone.

"What the hell—"

Lise whirled, raising the statue in front of her defensively. Then her arm fell to her side. "Judd," she quavered, "I—I thought you were a thief."

To her horror, a wave of faintness washed over her. Her knees buckled. She sank down on the bed, her breathing shallow in her throat, fighting back the red mist in her brain.

Judd flipped on a light switch. Then he knelt beside her, gently detaching her fingers from the statue. "Your hands are like ice," he said. "Lise, what the devil are you doing in my room?"

She flushed scarlet. "I heard something—it woke me. So I was going to call 911."

Judd said the obvious. "I got home early...what's the statue for?"

"To bash you on the head, of course."

"You're brave as a lion, you know that?"

He was still caressing her cold fingers; she stared at his

hands in fascination. "I was scared out of my wits," she confessed.

Raising her eyes, she looked full at him. He was still wearing an outfit much like the one she'd seen on TV; dark circles shadowed his eyes, and a long scrape ran from one wrist almost to his elbow. "Judd," she said, "I saw you on the TV news. In Sudan."

He swore under his breath, his jaw tight. "I was too busy arguing with the airport officials to even notice the media until it was too late. But I didn't figure it'd go international."

Again she stared absorbedly at his hands, feeling warmth creep back into her own. "Why didn't you tell me the truth? About your destination, I mean."

"I don't tell anyone I do that stuff." He paused, then added tautly, "I was in Venezuela doing airlifts the time of the fire. You can guess how I felt about that. But this time I knew Emmy would be safe with you. I trust you with her, Lise. Totally."

Moved to tears, Lise faltered, "The day you left, I accused you of being greedy and mercenary...I'm so sorry."

"You couldn't have known."

She looked up, gazing straight into his eyes. "You're a good man," she said unsteadily.

"I'm no angel, Lise. One reason I do it is for the risk, the adrenaline, the need to push my limits—nothing very saintly about that."

"You do it. That's what's important."

He shifted uncomfortably, releasing her hands. "I shouldn't be anywhere near you—I stink. No showers, and I was in too much of a hurry to get home to bother changing."

The words spoke themselves. "We could shower together," she said; and waited with bated breath for his response.

He stood up, pulling her to her feet. "You're wearing your sexy nightgown," he said, his features inscrutable. "Difficult for me to resist you in that."

"You see," she went on, as if he hadn't spoken, "I believe you. Not Angeline. I figured that out on Friday, the night I saw you on TV...I'm only sorry it took me so long."

"You're so generous," Judd said roughly. "You take my breath away."

With a radiant smile, Lise pulled his head down and kissed him full on the mouth. His stubble of beard rasped her chin; his response, instant and intense, soared through her body. Wasn't this why she'd taken the job as companion to Emmy? So she could be with Judd?

"Shower," he growled against her lips, nibbling them with erotic urgency. "I think I'll burn these clothes."

Sweeping her into his arms, he strode across the room to the bathroom, where a raised ceramic platform with a sunken Jacuzzi overlooked a small enclosed garden of pines and hemlocks. The shower was paneled in polished granite, with massage water jets at different levels; as Judd put her down and began stripping off his clothes, Lise stood still, almost faint with desire. When he was naked, he came over to her, easing her gown over her head, his gaze drinking in the gentle curves of her body. In quick distress, she said, "How did you scrape your arm? And you've got bruises all down your ribs."

He said awkwardly, "Getting one of the crew out of the crashed plane—we were afraid of fire, so we weren't being overly careful. Let's not talk about it, Lise, not now." He reached over to turn on the water and said with a boyish grin, "Last one in's a chicken."

As the jets pummeled her flesh, enveloping her in steam, Lise twisted her hair on top of her head. Judd advanced on her, the bar of soap in his hand, and suddenly she was laughing in exhilaration at the sheer joy of being with him again. She splashed him, her green eyes gleaming with mischief. He grabbed for her, running his hands down her body, then trapping her against the smooth tile and kissing her until she was breathless, boneless with longing. The pelt of dark hair on his chest was slick to his wet skin; water trickled from the concavity of his ribs to his navel. "You're so beautiful," she breathed.

His face intent, he cupped the weight of her breasts in his palms, stroking them to their tightened tips; and all the while he watched the play of expression on her face. In sudden impatience, he said, "I want you in my bed. Now."

"There's nowhere I'd rather be."

Swathing her in a towel, wrapping one around his hips, Judd led the way back into his room. Very gently he rubbed the water from her skin; then he began raining kisses on her lips, her throat and the silken slopes of her breasts. Smoothing her hips with long, rhythmic strokes, he drew them closer to his body, pressing her into his erection until she gasped with pleasure. They fell on the bed in a tangle of limbs. Judd's quickened breathing and heavily pounding heart echoed in her ears; she was encompassed by him, forgetful of anything in the world but him. She was where she belonged.

Then Judd reared up on one elbow. "Last time I didn't even think of protection. Not until the next day. Should I use something, Lise? Or are you—"

She stared at him blankly. She was pregnant. She didn't need protection. And now was the perfect time to tell him. She said faintly, "No, you don't need to use anything."

"I thought you were probably on the pill," he said with a crooked grin. "Should have asked, I know—but it all happened so fast in Dominica, I forgot all the normal rules."

The rules he used with other women, she thought sickly. Had they all been as willing as she? Falling into his bed like a ripe apple from a tree? Judd said urgently, "What's wrong? Why are you looking at me like that? Protection's an obvious issue, I'd have thought—I've never liked the idea of bringing an unwanted child into the world."

What of the child in her womb? Would he regard that as unwanted? Of course he would. Because Judd wasn't into commitment: he'd made that clear to her days ago. He'd been married once, and once was enough.

Then one more dimension of her dilemma tumbled into Lise's brain. If Judd were to find out she were pregnant, he'd probably insist on marrying her, to legitimize his child; she knew him well enough for that. So she'd have forced him into an unwanted marriage, a marriage he'd resent. As he would resent her, who was its pretext.

She couldn't—wouldn't—do that. Not for anything.

With the swiftness of panic, Lise twisted free of him, stumbling to her feet by the side of the bed. Crossing her arms over her breast, horribly aware of her nudity, she faltered, "I can't make love to you. I mustn't."

In a single lithe movement Judd rolled over and stood beside her, his body looming over hers. "What's going on, Lise?"

"We shouldn't be doing this. There's no future in it for either of us, we both know that. I'm sorry—I shouldn't have led you on the way I did, it was wrong of me."

"We're both adults. What happens between us in bed—it's unique and we'd be fools to pass it up."

"And that's where we're different," she said in sudden bitterness. "I'm a typical woman, the kind you read about in magazine articles—I can't have an affair with you just because the sex is great. Making love has to mean more than that! We're not in love, Judd—and you made it very clear you never want to fall in love again. So I'm pulling out now. Before I get hurt.''

He frowned. ''Are you saying you're falling in love with me?''

''No! I'm saying I don't want to risk that happening.'' In a low voice, she added, ''I'm not cool and sophisticated like all those other women you date. I could get hurt by you. And I'm not going to let that happen. That's what I'm getting at.''

In a sudden angry movement, Judd ripped the spread from the bed. ''Here, put this around you.''

She hugged the softly woven cloth to her body, grateful for its warmth, glad she was no longer naked. Knowing she'd never have a better opportunity, she added in a rush, ''I think I should leave before four months. It's not fair to Emmy for me to hang around.''

''You need the money.''

''I'll get another job—I can always do the course a year later.'' She'd have to anyway, because of the baby. But she couldn't tell him that.

''Stay,'' Judd said with sudden urgency, clasping her by the shoulders, all the force of his willpower in his words. ''Give us the chance to get to know each other better. Who knows—both of us might change.''

Briefly Lise was suffused with a hope as fragrant as rose petals. Or was it joy at the mere thought that Judd might change, might be open to more than just a passing affair?

Might fall in love with her? Might *want* to marry her?

But then her heart clenched with pain, hope crushed like a withered leaf. She couldn't stay, for the obvious reason that before long her pregnancy would reveal itself and become a weapon over Judd, a means to secure a hasty commitment that afterward he would regret. ''No,'' she said in a stony voice. ''I can't stay.''

His fingers dug into her shoulders with cruel strength.

"Then I'd suggest you start looking for another job right away," he said with icy precision. "Because you're right, Emmy's feelings are involved—she's starting to get fond of you. She doesn't need a second mother figure leaving her in the lurch."

Lise flinched. "You seem to be forgetting that you're the one who offered me this job."

"I haven't forgotten—it was one of the stupidest decisions I've ever made. Like I said, common sense goes out the window as far as you're concerned."

Once again he was looking at her as though he hated her. He certainly didn't look as though he had the remotest interest in making love to her anymore. Hugging her dignity as well as the bedspread, wondering if she could make it to the door without tripping and falling flat on her face, Lise said, "I'll do my best to be gone within the week."

"Fine," said Judd; and released her so suddenly she staggered.

Lise looped the spread to her knees and scuttled back to her own room. Closing the door, she collapsed on the bed. Her body ached with unfulfilled need and her soul felt bruised and battered. She'd been exiled. Exiled from Judd and from Emmy. Shut out from the possibility of happiness, all because her own body had betrayed her. What a cruel irony that the intimacy she'd shared with Judd was now banishing her from any hope of deeper intimacy.

Tomorrow she'd start looking into a move to Halifax. She couldn't stay in Montreal, the risk was too great of meeting Judd when her pregnancy was more advanced. Or after the baby was born. Either prospect made her shudder in terror.

But even worse would be a forced and loveless marriage. Anything was better than that.

CHAPTER ELEVEN

LISE was ready to leave the house at nine the next morning. She'd woken with a sore heart and a plan of action. She'd go to her apartment and do some more cleaning in the morning, then in the afternoon she'd get on the Internet at the library and start researching her move east. She'd feel better when she'd taken some action, she told herself stoutly, running down the stairs in her jeans and an old red sweater, pulling on her ski jacket as she went. The sooner she left here the better. For everyone.

By driving herself hard all morning, she got her bedroom and the bathroom stripped to the essentials; she was back at Judd's by quarter to twelve, in lots of time for Emmy. She was pulling off her jacket in the foyer when the doorbell rang. It was too early for Judd, who'd said he'd bring Emmy home from school for lunch. Swiftly Lise pulled the door open.

"Angeline!" she exclaimed, her face blank with shock.

"You should never wear red," Angeline said. "Didn't I teach you anything all those years ago?"

Horribly conscious that her hair was a mess and the red sweater none too clean because she'd been lugging bags of garbage to the basement of her apartment building, Lise said lamely, "Won't you come in?"

Angeline waved to the limousine parked in the driveway, then sauntered into the hallway, putting down the big package she was carrying. She was dressed in a sheared mink coat, dyed sapphire-blue; her cream wool pants and cashmere sweater were complemented by gleaming alligator boots. Her hair was an artful tumble of curls to her shoulders. She said calmly, as if she turned up on the door-step every other day, "Where's Judd? Not away, I hope."

"No. He should be here very shortly. With Emmy."

"My darling little Emmy...how is she?"

"Fine," Lise said baldly.

"And what are you doing here?" Angeline asked, wandering over to examine a Steuben bowl filled with tulips.

"I work here. As a companion to Emmy."

Angeline swung around, her pale blue eyes openly speculative. "Judd hired you?" Lise nodded. "How very odd," Angeline said. "I suppose he was grateful after the fire."

"I suppose he was," Lise said evenly. "I'm going to ask the same question—why are you here, Angeline? A surprise visit all the way from the Loire?"

"That's really none of your business."

Lise flushed; and to her relief heard a car pull up outside. The front door opened and Emmy burst through. She saw Lise first; shucking off her boots, she cried, "Guess what? The picture I drew last week of us tobogganing won a prize at the art show."

She flung her arms around Lise and hugged her. Lise's arms went around the little girl in a reflex response: a response she liked very much. Then she looked up and saw that Judd was watching them; and shivered from the open hostility in his gaze. He didn't want Emmy showing her such open affection, because he knew Lise was leaving as soon as she could. Then Judd's eyes swiveled sideways. He said in blank shock, "Angeline—what are you doing here?"

Emmy stiffened in Lise's embrace. She, too, looked over at the beautiful woman standing beside the tulips, a woman very much at her ease, who looked as though she owned the palatial foyer rather than being an uninvited guest. "I thought it was time I came to see my little daughter,'' Angeline said. "How are you, *ma chérie?*"

Emmy stood up straight, one hand clutching the hem of Lise's sweater. "I'm fine."

"Aren't you going to give *me* a hug?" Angeline asked with a winsome smile.

Obediently Emmy walked across the polished oak and stood as rigid as a doll while Angeline folded her in her arms. "I've brought you a present," Angeline said, indicating the package. "All the way from Paris."

"That's nice," said Emmy.

"Aren't you going to open it?"

Emmy undid the box, pulling out a very large, fluffy brown bear. "I already have a bear."

"That dreadful old thing you had four years ago?" Angeline shuddered delicately. "Time you threw it away, *ma petite.* This one's new and much bigger."

"But I love Plush."

For a moment Angeline looked less than doting. "You inherited your father's stubbornness, I see. This is a very expensive bear, Emmy, from the most exclusive toy shop in Paris."

Emmy said woodenly, "Thank you very much."

Smoothly Judd interrupted. "You might as well join us for lunch, Angeline. Emmy doesn't have long before she goes back to school. Lise, why don't you lead the way?"

So Lise, her hips swinging in her slim-fitting jeans, headed for the glass-enclosed solarium, where copper bowls of hyacinths and daffodils spilled glorious shades of azure and gold, filling the air with fragrance. Angeline was like a hyacinth, she thought: complex, extravagant and effortlessly beautiful. Had she really come to see Emmy? Or was her real aim Emmy's father?

As if he'd read her mind, Judd said, "I'm sure you had motives other than Emmy for coming this far, Angeline."

"They'll keep until later, darling."

Inwardly Lise winced. Judd said in an expressionless voice, "You never were any good at keeping secrets—and now is as good a time as any to tell me why you're here."

Angeline pouted her full lips. "You always could get anything out of me," she said gaily. "Old friends of Henri's live near here—Paul and Marie Gagnon...he's a retired bank president. They're having a gala concert in their home tomorrow night, some famous pianist or other. I'm invited, and I managed to get you on the list, too. I know it's very last minute, but you remember how I always loved spontaneity." Her smile, intimate and dazzling, hinted at other shared memories.

"The Gagnons—don't they have a son who used to be based in New York? Will he be there, Angeline?"

Angeline's laugh was brittle. "How would I know?"

With a touch of grimness, Judd added, "And where's Henri?"

"Doing something terribly important to the vineyard. But of course he'd never stop me from coming."

Judd said bluntly, "Get an invitation for Lise, and I'll go with you."

Angeline frowned, small lines marring her perfect forehead. "For Lise? Why?"

"She saved our daughter's life—or are you forgetting that? It's the least you can do."

Lise had been quiet long enough. If Judd thought she was going to tag along to some fancy party as an unwanted third, he could think again. "I don't want to go," she said with finality.

Judd's slate-gray eyes clashed with hers. "But I want you to," he said. "And I'm your employer—you'll go, Lise. It's an order."

She could quit. On the spot. "I have nothing to wear and no time to shop."

"Tomorrow morning. At Gautier's."

Gautier's was world famous for its designer label garments. "No," said Lise. "I can't afford Gautier's, even on the salary you're paying me. And I will not allow you to buy my clothes." Once had been more than enough.

"We'll leave at nine-thirty," Judd said.

He was treating her like a child. Or was he punishing her for leaving his employ? For refusing to make love to him? Her cheeks flushed with temper, Lise opened her mouth for a scathing retort, then noticed Emmy listening to this interchange with wide-held eyes. She clamped her lips shut. But Angeline had no such scruples. "Darling, Lise would be out of her depth...much kinder to leave her home with Emmy."

"The three of us go. Or you can go on your own," Judd said in a tone that brooked no argument.

Angeline's pout wasn't quite so decorative this time. "But who will stay with Emmy? Surely you wouldn't leave her here alone? Again."

"Maryann and her husband will stay with Emmy. And the Gagnons live only a few blocks from here...although your concern is very touching, Angeline."

Angeline had never been attuned to sarcasm. "Of course I'm concerned," she cooed. "Emmy's mine as much as yours."

Emmy chewed on her sandwich and said nothing, although Lise could see the child was picking up far more than the words that were being exchanged. Lise said, "If I'm as much out of my depth as you think I'll be, Angeline, I can always leave early."

"You'll leave when we're all ready to leave," Judd announced, his gray eyes inimical.

Lise glared at him and pointedly addressed herself to her croissant, which was smothered in avocado and shrimp and deserved more of her attention than it had been getting. Judd knew she wouldn't start an argument when Emmy was present. But Emmy wouldn't always be around; and she'd never liked dictators.

Angeline said sweetly, "You and I must have dinner at *Chez LaBelle,* Judd—for old times' sake. That was my favorite place, remember?"

He said impassively, "It went out of business six months ago. We'll have dinner here tomorrow evening."

"I may not be able to get an invitation for Lise," Angeline said with a touch of sharpness, "it's very late for that."

"Just mention my name," Judd said, "it'll work wonders. I've known Paul for years."

Lise chewed on a pickled onion. Judd wasn't acting like a man in love with his estranged wife; if he were, Lise was the last person he'd want tagging along to the gala. Or was he giving out the message he wasn't about to fall into Angeline's arms the moment she turned up?

What ordinary woman could compete with Angeline?

Judd started describing some of Emmy's accomplishments at school, drawing his daughter into the conversation; and eventually the meal was over. Emmy and Lise went upstairs to find some gym gear, Emmy staying behind to clean her teeth. Lise went back downstairs, her footsteps silent on the thick carpet. As she came around the corner she saw Angeline and Judd silhouetted against the tall windows that overlooked the driveway. Judd's back was to her. They were standing very close together, Angeline talking animatedly, Judd's attention focused on his beautiful ex-wife. Then Angeline pulled his head down and kissed him, her tapered fingers caressing the silky black hair at his nape.

Just so had she, Lise, caressed him. For a split second she was frozen to the spot. Then she backed up with frantic speed, her heart thrumming in her breast, her fingers ice-cold on the banister. She'd thought she'd known what jealousy meant the day Marthe had shown her the photos; but she'd known nothing. The pain that filled her body now was unlike anything she'd ever experienced. Unbearable. Unmendable.

Then Emmy came charging down the hall, her gym bag in one hand. "I'm going to be late—is Dad ready to take me back to school?"

With a valiant effort at normality, Lise said, "Give him a shout, I just need to go to my room for a minute."

She was being a coward. But she couldn't face Judd after what she'd seen. Hidden by the curve of the stairwell, she heard Emmy call out, and Judd's deep voice answer. Then Angeline purred, "I'd love to come and see your school, Emmy."

"All right," said Emmy with something less than enthusiasm.

The front door closed. Silence fell. Lise leaned against the nearest wall, hugging her arms to her body, wishing she'd never come to this big stone mansion that was owned by a man with a heart of stone. Last night Judd had wanted to make love to her, Lise. Today he was kissing his ex-wife.

If she had any sense, she'd run from here right now and never come back. But she couldn't do that to Emmy. If Judd had been telling the truth, Angeline had left her daughter without saying goodbye. She, Lise, couldn't do the same thing. It would be too cruel.

She was trapped.

Sharp at nine-thirty the following morning Lise presented herself at the front door. She was wearing her best wool skirt, of hunter-green, with leather boots and a matching hip-length green coat. Her chin was well up; her eyes openly unfriendly.

Judd said sardonically, "Good morning to you, too."

"Let's not pretend I'm doing this for fun, Judd. And don't push me, I can quit anytime."

"But you won't. Because of Emmy."

"Do you always use your opponent's weakest point as leverage?" she said bitterly.

"I do what it takes."

"Then let's go dress me up like some kind of mannequin. Who'll be on display tonight as one of Judd Harwood's two women."

"Is that how you see it?" he rapped.

"How else am I to see it?" Her temper got the better of her. "I saw you yesterday, kissing Angeline."

"She threw herself at me. That's what you saw."

"You weren't exactly struggling."

"You didn't hang around long enough."

"Why would I? To check out if your technique's the same with her as with me?"

His breath hissed between his teeth. "Watch it, Lise. Or I might be tempted to demonstrate my technique."

"Don't you dare!"

His answer was to clamp his arms around her, pull her toward him and kiss her hard on the mouth. Like a flash fire, Lise's anger flared into desire, hot, compelling and unquenchable. Then Judd as suddenly thrust her away. His chest heaving, he snarled, "I told you not to push me too far and that kiss had nothing to do with technique."

"No—it was about power! About winning. Because you can't bear to lose. Especially to a woman."

The morning sun pouring through the tall windows glinted in her hair and shot sparks from her brilliant eyes. Judd took a long, shuddering breath. "Maybe," he said harshly, "it was about feelings."

She wasn't going to go there; not with Judd. "Maybe it was about ownership."

His eyes narrowed. "Catch-22. If I don't kiss you, it's because I'm after Angeline. If I do, it's because I'm some kind of Don Juan. You've got it wrong about me winning all the time—with you, I can't."

The bitterness in his voice shocked Lise. If she weren't pregnant by him, might she have softened, asked him what he meant? But all her intuition screamed that if Judd knew she were pregnant, he would insist on marrying her: because it was his child she was carrying. His. Ownership indeed. She said in a toneless voice, "We'd better go. I want to be back for Emmy at lunchtime."

"Right. Emmy. She's your only concern, isn't she?"

"You're paying me to look after her."

"Do you love Emmy, Lise?"

Her jaw dropped. She remembered the fervor with which Emmy had hugged her this morning, the delicacy of the child's bones, her searching eyes and quick-witted grin. "I won't let myself—I can't afford to."

"Because you're hell-bent on vanishing from her life."

And what was she to say to that? *If you saw me in six months, you'd understand why?* Lise bit her lip and heard Judd say forcefully, "Lise, tell me what's bothering you."

"Nothing's bothering me, other than you. Judd, let's go."

"You've got to be the most infuriating woman I've ever met! Bar none."

"It's the red hair," she said flippantly. "Too bad it doesn't come out of a bottle. What color dress are you going to buy me this time?"

Briefly he reached out to stroke her vivid curls. "Naked is how I prefer you."

A fierce blush scorched her cheeks. With an indecipherable exclamation, Lise pushed open the door and saw the limo waiting for them, the chauffeur at the wheel. All the way downtown she sat in her own corner, staring out

the window. At Gautier's it came as no surprise that she
and Judd were ushered into a thickly carpeted private room
with two women to serve them. Lise disappeared into the
changing room, was supplied with an uplift bra, and was
eased into the first dress. It was black and frighteningly
elegant.

Feeling awkward and unsure of herself, she marched out
to the paneled, gilt-edged mirrors and Judd's discerning
eyes. He shook his head. "Not you, Lise."

It wasn't. He was right. She almost had to be poured
into the next dress, which was silver lamé with a price tag
that made her blanch. Before Judd could say anything, she
announced, "Marilyn Monroe I'm not. I don't want this
one."

"You'd stop traffic," he said, and winked at her.

A reluctant grin quirked her mouth. "Even if I can't sit
down."

Back in the changing room, Lise riffled through the rack
of dresses, beginning to enter into the spirit of the search;
neither black nor white became her, she hated pastels, and
anything red, orange or pink made her hair look like a
five-alarm fire. So that dispensed with a fair number of the
gowns. Then her hand stilled. The fabric was shot silk,
dark green with an iridescence of sapphire; the bodice
tight, the skirt paneled over a pencil-slim underskirt. She
said, "I'd like to try this one."

The saleswoman said, "Madame has good taste."

Which probably meant she'd picked the most expensive
dress on the rack. It was eased over her head. It fit perfectly, Lise knew that right away, and slipped her feet into
the high-heeled sandals the salon had provided. Her head
held high, she walked out of the changing room.

Judd got to his feet, his face intent. "That's it," he said.
"Perfect."

In silence Lise looked at her reflection, almost the re-

flection of a stranger: a tall, flame-haired woman whose
ivory shoulders supported narrow straps, and whose cleavage was a soft valley cupped by the stiff, dark silk. The
floating panels subtly emphasized the slit in the underskirt;
she looked elegant, sexy and very feminine. She'd never
worn a dress one-tenth as beautiful. And never would
again. Especially in the next few months.

"You'll need shoes to match," Judd said; and within
five minutes Lise had selected sandals whose narrow straps
made even her feet look sexy. Gossamer-thin stockings
were added, and toning makeup. Then Judd obtained a
swatch of the fabric and asked for everything to be deliv-
ered. Once Lise was in her street clothes again, he took
her by the arm. "Vaison's next," he said.

Vaison's was the local equivalent of Tiffanys in New
York. Lise said in alarm, "Whatever for?"

"The finishing touch," he said with a wolfish grin.

"Whatever you buy, I'm not going to keep," she said,
hands on her hips.

"You haven't seen it yet. So how do you know? And
I'm certainly not going to return it the next day—so you
might be stuck with it."

"You drive me crazy—you know that?"

"It's entirely mutual," Judd replied.

She looked at him through her lashes. "Wow—finally
we have something in common."

"Oh, we have more than that in common," he said, his
gaze skimming her body. "Here we are."

In Vaison's the level of personal attention Judd received
was again an eye-opener for Lise. He showed the swatch
of fabric, made a quick sketch of the neckline of her dress,
and said, "A pendant, I think. Something simple. Emeralds
and sapphires, perhaps?"

"I believe we have just the thing, *monsieur*."

The pendant brought from the vault was a single faceted

emerald flanked by two sapphires, the stones inset in gold and hung from a delicate gold chain. Lise, beyond speech, again looked at herself in the mirror and knew intuitively that it was the perfect jewelery for her gown. Emerald earrings were produced; as the salesman retreated to the vault again, she hissed, "Judd, you can't do this! What am I going to do—wear them when I'm grooming a dog? Or cleaning out cages? You mustn't! You've spent far too much money already."

"The dress needs jewelery," he said inflexibly. "You can sell them afterward. It'll help pay for your course."

"You can't give them to me! I won't let you."

"The women who come here generally don't argue with the men who—Lise, what's wrong?"

She was near tears. "This is a travesty," she said incoherently. "I really hate it, Judd."

"Travesty of what?" he demanded.

"Of what gift giving should be. Two people who care for each other choosing something the other will like. It's not one-sided. It's nothing to do with money and power. Don't you *see?*"

"Don't you like the pendant?"

"I love it. But that's not the point." As the salesman approached, she muttered, "Never mind. I knew you wouldn't understand," and stood by mutely as the jewels were wrapped and paid for. After Judd again requested delivery, he and Lise went outside. "I made a hair appointment for you at Gautier's, two-thirty," he said. "They'll give you a manicure as well."

People jostled her on the sidewalk; the sky was a heavy gray, the air milder and thick with rain to come. Lise felt very tired. She said, "I've had enough of this. More than enough. I'm going to walk home, I need to be alone for a while. But I'll be there for Emmy at lunchtime."

"Lise," Judd said deliberately, "about the pendant.

Seeing you at home with Emmy, whose life you saved, is gift enough for me. Watching the two of you play in the snow or share a joke together…nothing you could buy me can equal that. And emeralds are nothing in comparison.''

She gazed at him in silence. She wanted to bawl her head off, she wanted to scream and yell and stamp her feet; as if she were three years old, not twenty-eight. ''I— I'll see you this evening,'' she muttered.

''I want you to know something else. It's very clear to me—it always has been—that you're not one bit interested in my money.'' He gave her a crooked grin. ''I like that. Very much.''

The wind ruffled his black hair; his smile made her heart melt. The words tumbled out before she could stop them. ''The way we were in bed—that had absolutely nothing to do with money.''

''I may be like a bull in a china shop where you're concerned, but I did understand that much.''

''I can't imagine why I said that. This is a crazy conversation.''

''Maybe it's a real conversation.''

As she made an indecipherable sound, Judd rested his hands on the shoulders of her jacket. ''The pendant—I want you to keep it, Lise. Three stones, an emerald and two sapphires. Think of Emmy and you and me—there might so easily have been no emerald.''

But you and I—we're not a couple. We're not a matched pair of sapphires. ''Oh,'' she said.

''Will you keep it? It's important to me that you do.''

Her green eyes were full of confusion. ''I—I guess so.''

He kissed her swiftly on both cheeks. ''Good. Off you go, or you'll be late for lunch, and I'll miss my conference call.''

He turned, walking back in the direction of the parked limo. Lise set off the other way. Just when she had Judd all figured out, he said something that threw her, that made her see him in a different light. As a result of which, she'd just accepted a hugely expensive gift from a man who didn't know she was carrying his child. She was purposely deceiving him, and simultaneously accepting jewels of a beauty and extravagance beyond her imagining.

Jewels and gratitude, she thought with painful honesty. That was all Judd was offering her. Along with a healthy dose of lust.

He wasn't offering love. Or commitment.

CHAPTER TWELVE

AT EIGHT o'clock that evening Lise was dressed and ready for the gala. She and Emmy had shared supper on a tray in Lise's room, and Emmy was now curled up on Lise's bed along with Plush; the bear Angeline had given her was conspicuous by its absence. As Lise put the finishing touches to her makeup, Emmy said with undoubted sincerity, "You look like a fairy princess."

The one who gets the prince? But the prince didn't want her. Or, at least, only in his bed.

Maybe, just maybe, this dress would change his mind?

The thought had come from nowhere. *I don't want Judd,* Lise thought in panic. *I don't love him. Of course I don't.*

Or do I? Would I give a hundred pendants to have him hold me in his arms and tell me he loves me?

She dragged her attention to the mirror. Her hair was piled high on her head, exposing the creamy length of her throat; the dress fit her like a glove, its shimmer of dark greens and blues subtly emphasizing the deep green of her eyes. The pendant glittered above her cleavage, while the earrings sparkled and shone. She looked poised and very elegant.

The poise was fake.

But the dress was real. Could it, perhaps, make Judd look at her with new eyes? Eyes that went deeper than her body?

The body that was carrying his child. She didn't want her baby to be fatherless; she herself had loved her father deeply, and had missed his steadfast presence for years.

So was that it? She wanted Judd simply so her child would have a father?

With her usual incurable honesty, Lise knew she was evading the truth. She wanted Judd for himself. Body and soul. She wanted his ardor, his tenderness, his laughter and intensity. For herself. As well as for her child. So was that love?

Emmy said with a pleasurable shiver, "You look like you've just seen a ghost."

Lise's gaze jerked back to the little girl on the bed. "I—I was daydreaming."

"I bet my dad will think you look like a princess, too."

"Your mother will outshine me, Emmy."

"But you're nicer," Emmy said naively.

Lise fought down a smile. "Thank you for putting the pendant on for me," she said; she'd found the clasp too intricate to manage on her own.

"It's jazzy. Dad must like you a lot to give it to you."

Lise said gently, "He's grateful to me, Emmy, that's all. You mustn't build castles in the air."

Which is precisely what she herself had been doing.

Tomorrow, she thought. Tomorrow she must somehow break the news to Emmy that she'd be leaving very soon. That she was moving away and severing any connection between the two of them. She dreaded it. But it had to be done, and done with all the sensitivity and care she could muster.

"I'd better go down," Lise said, "it's time to leave."

Emmy bounced off the bed and tucked her hand in Lise's. "I'll come, too."

To feel Emmy's warm fingers curled around her own was the most bittersweet of sensations. She loved Emmy. No question of that. It was going to hurt horribly to say goodbye to her. Pushing these thoughts aside, Lise smiled down at the little girl. "Thanks for all your help."

So when Lise descended the circular staircase to the foyer, where an austerely designed Belgian chandelier cast pools of golden light, she had Emmy's moral support to give her courage. Judd and Angeline were standing at the foot of the stairs waiting for her. Judd looked startlingly handsome in a tuxedo and pleated white shirt; as for Angeline, her silver gown made her look like a real princess: the one who did get the prince, Lise thought with a wrench at her heartstrings.

Judd said spontaneously, "You look magnificent, Lise."

His smile was so high voltage that Lise felt her fragile composure tremble. "Thank you...how are you, Angeline?"

Angeline was staring at Lise as if she'd never seen her before; when she noticed the pendant, she looked like a schoolgirl who's just found out someone else has beaten her to first prize. "I presume Judd chose your dress," she said with the nearest thing to malice she was capable of. "He always did have good taste."

"Actually I picked it out on my own," Lise replied.

Angeline produced the moue made famous on many a billboard. "We're getting my mother on the way to the Gagnons', she's coming, too. She was wrong when she said you'd never be beautiful like me."

It was impossible to dislike Angeline, Lise thought ruefully; although the prospect of Judd and Marthe in the same car made her shudder. "That's very generous of you," she said, and meant it.

Angeline glanced over at her daughter. "I'd love a hug, *petite*—although don't muss my dress."

Emmy complied dutifully. Then she said, "You look cool, Dad."

Judd picked her up and swung her high over his head. "Thanks, sweetheart. You'll be fine with Maryann, she's going to stay in the guest wing all night."

"She said I could watch TV until nine-thirty."

"Just go easy on the chocolate-coated popcorn."

I wish I was staying home and watching TV, Lise thought. And fifteen minutes later when Marthe, in ice-blue satin, joined them in the limo, wished it even more sincerely. Marthe was frigidly polite to Judd, overly solic-itous with her daughter and, after one affronted look that took in the designer gown and the jewels, ignored Lise completely.

That was fine with Lise. There were enough potential pitfalls in the evening ahead without adding Marthe's acid tongue. Nevertheless, she couldn't suppress a quiver of anticipation when they drew up outside the Gagnons' huge—and, in her opinion, hugely ugly—medieval-style castle. Pillars, archways, buttresses and turrets, it had them all. As for the inside, she swiftly gained an impression of a decorator-perfect and soulless house, with none of the individuality of Judd's eclectic collection of cherished ob-jects.

The Gagnons, however, were gray-haired, rotund and friendly; their only son, Roland, who was visiting from New York, was blond and sleekly handsome. He kissed Angeline, whom he obviously knew, on both cheeks, gave Judd a look of cool assessment that rather puzzled Lise and shook Lise's hand with enthusiasm. "Delighted to meet you," he said, his boyish grin laden with charm. And just before the concert began in an anteroom to the elegant ballroom, he slipped into the seat next to Lise. She'd man-aged—rather successfully, she thought—to lose Judd and Angeline in the crush; and Roland's company was cer-tainly preferable to Marthe's.

"Didn't think I'd ever get to stop shaking hands," he whispered. "Once this is done, the dancing begins. Real music."

"You don't like classical music?"

"It's okay if you're over sixty-five. The Viennese waltz crowd will be in the ballroom after this concert's over. But the real action—disco and hip-hop—will be in the great room at the back of the house. I want to dance with you, Lise."

"Thank you," she said limpidly. "How do you know Angeline?"

"Oh, I met her a couple of years before she left for France," he said vaguely. "What's with you and Judd?"

"He's my employer." As Roland gave her a knowing look, Lise added more sharply than she'd intended, "I look after his daughter."

"Okay, okay...oops, here comes the piano player. I'd better shut up, Mum can't stand it when I talk through her kind of music. What's the difference, I say, cover one kind of noise with another." He grinned. "Makes her very cranky."

Roland might be a lightweight, thought Lise, but at least he was keeping her mind off the way Angeline had been commandeering Judd's attention all evening. She inspected her gilt-embossed program, settling down to enjoy herself as best she could. The pianist was world-class and the music did calm her; but afterward Judd tracked her down, insisting she accompany him, Angeline and Marthe to the ballroom, where an orchestra was tuning its instruments and white-jacketed waiters were passing champagne and delicious hors d'oeuvres. Roland vanished, having promised to rescue her in half an hour. With grim determination, Marthe engaged Lise in conversation.

So it was Angeline Judd led onto the dance floor first. They made a strikingly handsome couple, Lise thought with a painful twist of her heart; despite her own beautiful dress and her jewels, Judd had been nothing but punctiliously polite to her. Wishing she was sitting on her perch at the back of the fire truck, where at least she'd know who she was, she said, "Angeline looks lovely, Marthe."

Marthe said in a staccato voice, "She's left the count. She's coming home to stay. She and Judd will remarry. For Emmy's sake."

Some champagne slopped from Lise's glass onto the skirt of her dress. Her lashes flew down to hide her eyes. Of course. Why hadn't she guessed there was a motive behind Angeline's sudden appearance? And that it would be tied in with Emmy?

Angeline and Judd a couple again. Angeline, Judd and Emmy a family.

Her fingers trembling, Lise scrubbed at the damp stain on her dress. In a totally artificial voice, she said, "Look what I've done, how silly of me. Please excuse me, Marthe, I'll try toweling it dry in the ladies' room."

She pushed back her chair. The myriad lights from the crystal chandeliers blurred in her vision; frantically she held back tears that if they once started might never stop. Asking one of the waiters for directions, she fled the ballroom.

The washroom was adorned with vases of red roses in front of gold-framed mirrors. Perhaps she could hide in here for the rest of the evening, Lise thought crazily. At least Judd couldn't come after her.

He wasn't going to come after her. He was going to remarry Angeline, Emmy's mother. Thank God she, Lise, had had the sense to keep her pregnancy to herself. But what would it be like giving birth to Judd's child and knowing that Judd was forever lost to her?

Other women came and went, chattering and laughing. Eventually Lise got up, repaired her lipstick and headed for the great room where strobe lights flashed and the heavy beat of the bass throbbed through her body. As she edged further into the room, Roland waved at her. "Been looking everywhere for you,'' he said. ''Even braved the ballroom, how about that? Let's dance.''

Anything was better than the numb despair that had her in its grip. So Lise began to dance, her limbs feeling heavy and awkward. The noise level was too loud for conversation; the pulsing lights both hid and revealed her.

When the band stopped for a break, Roland led her toward the buffet table, which was laden with an array of food that at any other time would have taken her breath away. She was picking at some tiger shrimp when she saw, across the width of the room, Judd's broad shoulders. She ducked behind another couple, but it was too late: he'd seen her. She could run, once more, for the washroom. But a stubborn kind of pride kept Lise where she was.

He strode up to her; in the intermittent light, she saw that he was in a towering rage. He rasped, ''Where the hell have you been?''

''Dancing. With Roland.'' Who, she noticed, was applying himself to his braised scallops as if Judd didn't exist.

''It's time you danced with me.''

''I don't think so, Judd. You may have clothed me. But you don't own me.''

His breath hissed between his teeth. ''I've danced with Angeline twice. I've danced with her mother, which was an interesting experience. I've danced with Roland's mother and two of his sisters. And now I'm going to dance with you.''

''I don't want to dance with you!''

He took her by the arm, his fingers digging into her bare flesh. ''We'll discuss this somewhere else.''

Briefly Lise contemplated staging a full-blown scene. It was tempting; it might even make her feel better. But the Gagnons had welcomed her with genuine hospitality, and Roland had been kind to her in his own way; they deserved better of her than that. "Let go of me," she said. "I'll come of my own free will or not at all."

Unwilling admiration flickered over Judd's face. "You've got spirit, I'll give you that," he said, and slid his hands with lingering sensuality down her arms to her wrists. Lightly clasping the fingers of one hand, he raised them to his lips, and kissed them one by one.

Lise stood rooted to the spot, fury and desire exploding in her veins. She snatched her hand back, said to Roland, "I'll be back. Very soon," and marched across the dance floor. But before she could reach the far side of the room, the percussionist struck three heavy chords, and the band picked up the beat. She pivoted to face Judd. "You wanted to dance. Then dance."

The beat echoed the racing of her heart. She threw herself into the music, moving her body with overt sensuality and no caution whatsoever. Pouring her turmoil of emotion into the music, she danced as she'd never danced before, her eyes glittering, her hips gyrating, her cheeks flushed from far more than exertion. The whole length of the song, Judd's eyes never left her, as in pagan invitation she flaunted herself in front of him. The song ended in a flourish from the electric guitars. Judd whirled her into the circle of his embrace and kissed her full on the mouth.

Lise melted into him, kissed him back and from a long way away heard a chorus of wolf whistles. Abruptly Judd pushed her away. "We've got an audience," he drawled. "Too bad."

He looked thoroughly in control of himself and of the situation. Whereas Lise felt as limp as a rag doll. In a cracked voice she said, "Are you happy? You've had your dance. Now you can go back to Angeline."

"What if I don't want to?"

"I think you do…I know you do. Regardless, let me spell something out." She took a deep breath, only wanting this to be over. "I'm not another option, Judd. I never have been and never will be."

In a voice like ice, Judd said, "Are you telling me the truth, Lise? Think about it very carefully before you answer."

He'd given her her chance; and she had no choice, she had to take it. Because she was pregnant with his child. "Yes, it's the truth," she said steadily. "I'll tell Emmy tomorrow that I'm leaving, and I'll be gone right after that."

"Fine," Judd said, turned on his heel and threaded his way toward the entrance.

Lise watched him go, standing as though turned to stone in the middle of the dance floor. Judd wouldn't be back, not this time. He'd go straight to Angeline. Who'd welcome him with open arms.

She'd done it. And what a place, Lise thought wildly, to realize your heart's broken.

The next song started. Once again she ran for the ladies' room, this time searching her evening bag and discovering she had more than enough money to get a cab back to Judd's house. That's what she'd do. And in the morning she'd tell Emmy she was leaving right away. A clean break. A new start.

She could do it. She was known for her courage, wasn't she?

She'd rather face a burning warehouse full of explosives than either Emmy or Judd. And that really was the truth.

Fifteen minutes passed. Feeling ten years older, Lise pushed herself to her feet. Twelve hours from now she'd be back in her apartment; and a week from now, with any luck, she'd be on her way to Halifax.

She could do it. Because she had to.

Her face pale, she walked back into laughter, music and the buzz of conversation. The Gagnons should be pleased;

the party was a success. All she had to do was find a phone and she'd be out of here.

"Hey," said Roland, "you looking for me?"

"Roland, will you call me a cab?" she asked with the directness of desperation. "I—I've got a headache. But I don't want Judd to know I'm leaving."

"Oh," Roland said easily, "that's no problem. He and Angeline just left. They took off in a taxi. For Angeline's hotel, I think that's what she said."

For a horrifying moment, the room dipped and swayed. I won't faint, Lise thought with fierce concentration. I won't. Holding onto the one thing she knew, she repeated, "A cab, Roland? Please?"

"Sure—you don't look so great. But you won't mind if I stay here?"

Roland, she was almost sure, would have another pretty girl in tow before half an hour was up; while she herself craved to be alone. "Of course not."

Calling on all her good manners, Lise made her fare-wells to her host and hostess, and allowed Roland to escort her under an umbrella to the taxi. It was raining, the wind blowing gusts of drops across the wide driveway. She scrambled into the cab and Roland slammed the door shut. Lise gave Judd's address and sank back against the seat. Too distraught to think, she blanked from her mind any thought of what Judd was doing now. Judd and Angeline.

She'd have lots of time for that. And how could she blame Judd? She'd given him the brush-off loud and clear. That he'd run so quickly to Angeline was nothing to do with her and everything to do with his proposed remarriage.

Minutes later she was running upstairs in Judd's house, holding her skirts up so as not to trip. Maryann was already in bed; Emmy was fast asleep, three books and Plush spread over the covers. Lise stood in the doorway, feeling

yet another crack open in her heart. How could she so
quickly have come to love Emmy?

This was the last night she'd ever stand here like this,
listening to Emmy's breathing, a little girl whose life she
had saved and who had thereby utterly changed her own
life.

Quickly Lise went into her own room. The jeans and
shirt she'd been wearing earlier in the day were still flung
on the bed. Ordinary clothes. The kind that she'd be wearing from now on. Impulsively she kicked off her elegant
sandals and reached for the zipper on her gown, frantic to
be rid of it and all it stood for; and a couple of minutes
later, wearing her jeans and shirt, was yanking the pins
from her hair, brushing it until it stood in a cloud from her
face. The emerald earrings she flung on the bureau; but
once again the clasp on the pendant defeated her.

Scarcely thinking, Lise pulled on her rain jacket and
rubber boots and dropped the front door key in her pocket.
She'd go for a walk. She couldn't stand to go tamely to
bed, where she'd be alone with feelings and thoughts she
wasn't sure she could face. She'd always loved storms.
And a little rain wouldn't hurt her. The last thing she
picked up was the flashlight that was stored in the drawer
in her bedside table.

The wind howling along the driveway buffeted her so
hard she had to lean into it, while rain drove its cold pellets
into her face. Lise didn't care. Now that she was finally
alone, she was free to weep, for tears would mingle with
the rain trickling down her cheeks; but the desolation in
her heart was too profound for that. At some deep level
she felt betrayed.

Judd had made love to her; and now was making love
with Angeline. How *could* he?

Head down, eyes almost shut, she ploughed along. She
had no idea what she was going to do when she reached

the main road. Turn around and go meekly to bed? Walk the deserted streets until she was exhausted? She'd decide when she got there, she thought, and was almost glad to feel the pull in her muscles from the exercise.

Her flashlight made a small puddle of light on the wet black tar. Lise switched it off, letting her eyes adjust to the darkness; she was easily able to discern the edge of the driveway. Branches rattled in the wind, which thrashed the boughs of the tall pines and hemlocks. If she closed her eyes, she could almost imagine she was beside the ocean, listening to the hiss of waves, the crash of surf against the rocks...

Light suddenly shone against her closed lids, brilliant and unforgiving. Her eyes flew open. A car was hurtling toward her up the driveway, the headlights throwing long gold beams through the wet trees. Then the driver sighted her and in a scream of brakes the car ground to a halt scarcely ten feet away from her. It was the limo. Lise stood still, feeling as though her heart had leaped into her throat. The driver's door opened and Judd lunged out.

Judd. The last person in the world she wanted to see.

CHAPTER THIRTEEN

GLANCING from side to side like a cornered animal, Lise took to the trees. But her hands were too cold to turn the flashlight on, and once she left the circle of light thrown by the car, she was in utter darkness. Her boot caught in a root. She almost fell, saving herself by grabbing at the nearest trunk. The baby. She had to think of the baby. She couldn't risk losing it by running through the woods in the middle of the night.

With a sob of frustration, Lise turned around and waited for Judd to catch up with her. His flashlight wavered through the undergrowth. Twigs cracked underfoot. He stopped only a foot from her and shone the light full in her face. "You little idiot—I could have killed you! What in heaven's name are you doing out on a night like this without even a flashlight?"

Lise said with icy calm, "I have a flashlight. And you're the last person I was expecting to see. Where's Angeline? In the car waiting for you? So you can go to bed with her?"

He dropped his flashlight to the ground and took Lise by the shoulders. "What the devil's Angeline got to do with this? Don't you understand? I came as near to running you over as I ever—"

In the dim glow of light, Lise saw that he was white about the mouth; and somehow this was the spark that ignited her rage. "If you expect me to apologize, you're going to wait a long time," she seethed. "And you're not stupid, Judd, you know as well as I do that Angeline's got everything to do with this. But do you know what's so awful? That I had to come back here at all. That I can't leave tonight because tomorrow morning I have to tell Emmy I'm going—I won't let someone else tell her, I couldn't stand to have that on my conscience. I can't even risk running away in the woods! I'm trapped. And I never wanted to see you again. Never, do you hear?''

She seemed to have run out of words. Her nails were digging into the bark of the tree trunk, rather like Judd's fingers were digging through her jacket. He said in an odd voice, ''Why can't you risk running through the woods? You're not scared of the dark or the storm—or you wouldn't be out in the first place.''

She was sick to death of deception. And she had nothing left to lose. Lise said flatly, ''Because I'm pregnant.''

''What?''

''You heard. I'm pregnant. By you.''

The wet plume of a hemlock brushed Judd's shoulder. He didn't even notice. After a silence that seemed to last forever, he said in voice Lise had never heard before, ''You weren't on the pill in Dominica.''

''Why would I be? There wasn't a man in my life. Dave was just a friend.''

''So when we nearly made love here, you were already pregnant. No need for protection.''

''That's right,'' Lise said, and with a distant part of her brain realized how relieved she was to have the truth in the open. ''I should have told you then. But I was afraid to.''

''The day you fainted—that was why.''

''Yes.'' In a rush she went on, ''You don't have to worry, I won't make any claim on you. Or on your money. I've given up my apartment and I'm going to move to the East Coast. Next week if I can swing it. Emmy will never know, and as for you and Angeline, you can both forget all about me.''

She couldn't have disguised the bitterness she felt. With none of his usual economy of movement, Judd bent and picked up the flashlight, shining it in her face again. She stared back, hostility masking any other emotion; and was glad she hadn't wept. He didn't deserve her tears.

A sudden gust ripped through the trees, driving rain straight at her. Instinctively Lise ducked. Swiftly Judd pulled her closer, shoving the light in his pocket as he sheltered her with his big body. He was wearing a raincoat over his tuxedo; to her nostrils drifted the scent of his cologne.

It was the final straw. Filled with a chaos of rage, longing and pain, Lise beat on his chest with her fists. "Let go! How dare you even touch me? I hate you, Judd Harwood—I hate you!"

A shudder ran through his body. He pushed her away, his eyes like dark pits in his face. "We're going to the house and have this out, Lise. Now."

"I'm not getting into the limo with Angeline!"

"For God's sake," he exploded, "Angeline's back in her hotel. Nowhere near here. Are you going under your own steam or do I have to pick you up and carry you?"

"I can still walk," she flared. "I'm pregnant—not breakable." Only her heart was broken, she thought wretchedly, and realized that deep down she must have cherished a fantasy of telling Judd she was pregnant and of having him enfold her in his arms and promise to love her forever.

Just like in the fairy tales.

Judd swung the flashlight to show their path, and led the way out of the trees. When he opened the passenger door, he must have seen how Lise's gaze flickered to the back of the empty limo before she climbed in. He said savagely, "You don't believe one word I say, do you?"

"Why should I?"

He slammed the door and moments later climbed in beside her, putting his foot on the accelerator so they raced up the driveway. The wipers swished away the curtain of rain; the house looked dark and ominous, a black bulk against the sky. Lise huddled in her seat. She felt cold and very tired. Yet one piece of information kept circling her exhausted mind. Angeline was back at her hotel.

What did that mean? And was it true?

Judd pulled to a halt by the front door. She climbed out before he could come around to open her door, and headed up the steps. Judd unlocked the door. The warmth brushed her cheeks as tangibly as a caress, and she began to shiver.

Judd said roughly, "You're soaked. Come on upstairs and I'll start a bath for you."

She had to know. "Why did you leave the Gagnons' party with Angeline?"

"We're not going to have that discussion while you're dripping on the carpet like a drowned rat."

"Are you going to marry her?"

With an impatient exclamation, Judd pushed her in the direction of the stairs. "What in hell would I do that for?"

"For Emmy's sake. Of course."

"I am not now or ever going to remarry Angeline. Once was enough, thank you. And you can take that to the bank." He took Lise by the elbow, hurrying her up the stairs. "I wouldn't marry her for my sake or for Emmy's sake. Emmy loves *you,* Lise—her mother's a stranger to her. Now where do you keep that disgraceful old nightgown you've had for seventeen years? It looks like this is the night to wear it."

He wasn't going to marry Angeline. "Is that the truth, Judd?" Lise whispered.

He stopped dead at the top of the stairs; she felt the force of his willpower like a blast of sheer energy. "Lise, I may have lied to you by omission, but never by commission. Yes, it's the truth. I'm no longer in love with Angeline, and I have no desire whatsoever to marry her.''

"Oh," said Lise, and discovered she was shivering again.

Judd suddenly swept her up into his arms. "I was in control until I met you," he said in a raw voice. "I had women figured out, and my life was just the way I wanted it. Straight track all the way to the horizon, all signals go. Then I meet up with a female firefighter with hair like flame and a temper to match, and I'm off the rails. Explain that to me, will you?''

She couldn't. She was too busy fighting the temptation to bury her face in his wet raincoat and sob her heart out. But she wasn't going to do that.

Not yet.

In short order Judd put her down beside her bed and marched into the bathroom to fill the Jacuzzi. He came back to find her standing exactly where he'd left her. He said levelly, "I've turned the heat up in the bathroom. Where's your nightgown?''

"Second drawer down.''

He pulled it out and threw it on the bed. Then he walked over to Lise and drew down the zipper of her jacket, a small gesture that woke in her an agony of memories. She flinched away from him. His hand froze partway down. He said, "You do hate me, don't you? You can't even stand to have me near you.''

How was she to answer that? As her lashes fell, hiding her eyes, she told the literal truth. "I don't know anything anymore.''

"Go have your bath," Judd said. "Once you're warmed up, you should get some sleep.''

His voice was devoid of emotion. All her movements like those of a robot, Lise yanked down her zipper, passed him her soaked jacket and walked past him to the bathroom, picking up her nightgown on the way. Closing the door, she stripped off the rest of her clothes and got in the tub.

The hot water laved her skin; she sank down in it, turned on the jets and floated boneless as a doll. Gradually she began to feel warmer. And with warmth came emotion, and with emotion the awakening of a desperate need for truth.

She had to know what had happened tonight. Judd no longer loved Angeline and didn't want to marry her. That, however, wasn't the same as saying he'd fallen in love with Lise. Yet she'd disrupted his life, thrown it off the rails. Whatever that meant.

Was he worth fighting for?

Wasn't that the real question? Nothing to do with Angeline, and in a very real way nothing to do with the baby in her womb. It was a question for her, Lise. For her and for Judd. Because, of course, she loved Judd. Through and through, with all her heart. Had done for weeks.

Dazedly Lise watched the ripples and bubbles in the hot water, and discovered that she was smiling with pure joy. Why had it taken her so long to admit that simple, earth-shattering truth? Hadn't it been her hidden love that had impelled her to tell him she was pregnant? To stop deceiving him about something that was of utter significance to both of them? No matter what happened.

Swiftly she leaned forward and turned off the taps. Then she climbed out onto the bath mat, pulled a towel from the rack and wrapped it around her. The pendant Judd had given her was nestled between her breasts. One emerald and two sapphires, the colors of leaves and of water: the colors of life. Still smiling, Lise pulled the door open.

The bedroom was empty.

For a moment she stood transfixed, feeling terror pluck at her composure. Was she being an utter fool to think

Judd wanted anything more of her than he'd already had? That he might, given time, come to love her not as the mother of his child, but as herself?

There was only one way to find out.

On bare feet she tiptoed down the hallway. His bedroom door was shut. Biting her lip, she very slowly turned the handle and eased the door open, all in total silence.

Judd was sitting on the edge of his bed, his back to her, his head buried in his hands. He'd stripped to his black trousers; the line of his spine was a long curve of defeat, all his arrogance and pride gone.

She couldn't bear to see him like that.

Lise slipped through the doorway and just as softly closed it behind her. As the latch clicked, Judd's head jerked up. He looked over his shoulder, saw her standing there and pushed himself to his feet. "Lise," he said hoarsely, "what are you doing here?"

"I had to come," she gulped. "I need to know what happened tonight with Angeline. I need to know how you feel about me carrying your child—please, Judd, won't you tell me?"

His jaw was tight and there were dark shadows under his eyes. Lise found she was holding her breath, her pulse racketing in her chest. The rest of her life depended on what happened next, she was under no illusion about that. Praying desperately that he wouldn't shut her out, she waited for him to speak.

He crossed the room. "You're still wet."

"I—I guess I am," she said lamely.

"And you're still wearing the pendant."

"I can't undo the catch, it's too small. But I—"

He said, "Angeline came running up to me after I left you on the dance floor at the Gagnons. There'd been an emergency with Emmy, she'd fallen down the stairs and was crying for me. I wasn't about to question one more emergency, not after the fire. Angeline had a cab all lined up—so off we went, top speed, Angeline filling me in with all the details...until I happened to look out the window of the cab and see we were going in the wrong direction. Well, you can probably guess the rest. No emergency. No fall down the stairs. Angeline had decided to take me to her hotel and seduce me. Step one in the remarriage campaign."

"That's where Roland told me you'd gone," Lise said. "To her hotel. Together."

"So that's why you ran off into the woods—"

"Wouldn't you?"

"Roland is the lover Angeline had in New York while she and I were still married. No doubt, for old times' sake, she asked him to pass along that message to you." His voice gravelly with anger, Judd said, "I'm sorry, Lise. How could you possibly have known what was really going on?"

Remembering the way Roland had been so cool with Judd, Lise said, "It seems very obvious about Roland— now that I do know."

"Let me finish with Angeline. The count's dumped her, to put it crudely. An indiscretion on her part. Unfortunately, Henri wasn't amused, and chose not to forgive his wife for having an affair with one of his best friends. So Angeline, who's used to living in the lap of luxury, decides I'm not such a bad deal after all, and comes hightailing back to Montreal with marriage on her mind. All for Emmy's sake, you understand." He ran his fingers through his hair. "I took her to her hotel in the cab, went right back to the Gagnons to look for you, discovered you'd left and raced back here in the limo. End of story."

"Marthe told me Angeline had done the leaving and was planning to remarry you."

"Poor Lise. Everyone telling you everything but the truth."

"You really don't want Angeline?"

"I do not. It's you I want, Lise."

She swallowed. "The way you wanted me in Dominica?"

Briefly he rested his finger where the pulse beat at the base of her throat. He said huskily, "I'll never stop wanting you that way."

But that's not enough. Lise said carefully, "So you're still not into commitment. Let alone marriage."

"You're pregnant. Of course we'll get married."

"No, Judd—I won't marry you just because I'm pregnant. The child and I both deserve better than that."

"The child deserves a father."

"Any child deserves a father. But if the parents don't love each other, the marriage is flawed from the start. I can't do that, Judd, I just can't."

"You don't love me," he said in an unreadable voice. "That's what you're saying."

She tilted her chin. "You don't love me. So why should it matter to you how I feel?"

"I told you I've lied by omission," Judd said with sudden violence. "I had no intention of showing you in Dominica what our lovemaking meant to me. How deeply it affected me, body and soul. I wasn't into commitment—you're right. So why would I say that your beauty and generosity had knocked me sideways, had made me re-examine the way I've been living the last four years? That I was starting to want you in all the ways a man wants a woman? In his bed every night, waking up beside him in the morning…I wasn't going to tell you that, Lise, because it scared the hell out of me."

"If we got married just because of the baby," Lise said deliberately, "how long before you started to resent me?

Underpaid Firefighter Traps Millionaire Into Marriage Of Convenience. It's classic. And I won't do it.''

"It's my child, too. We're both responsible."

He sounded so reasonable, so cold-blooded. She said raggedly, "I'll move away as soon as I can. I promise I won't make any—"

"Lise, hold on, I'm doing this all wrong." Judd took her in his arms, his eyes running over the gentle slopes of her shoulders to where the pendant sparkled in the valley between her breasts. "Why did you come here like this? Half-naked and so beautiful I can hardly think straight?"

She tried to pull the towel higher. "It was stupid of me, I didn't stop to think."

He stayed her hand. "When you came around that door, I was sitting on the edge of the bed convinced I'd lost you. Forever. That the woman I want to spend the rest of my life with hated my guts."

"But—"

"Yes, I was scared in Dominica, you'd turned my life upside down and I've always been into control. Lise, don't you see? I'm trying to tell you I love you. I was in love with you in Dominica, I probably fell in love with you when I first saw you lying in that hospital bed. I love you and I want to marry you. But if—"

"Not just because of the baby?" she blurted.

"I want to marry you for yourself. But how can I ask you to do that when you told me out in the woods that you hate me?"

"You love me," she repeated blankly.

"All I'm asking is that you stick around," he said with repressed violence. "Stay here with me and Emmy. Because I can't stand the thought of you moving away. Of us being separated by half a continent."

"I won't move away. Why would I do that?" Lise's

smile broke through, as radiant as sunrise. "You see, I love you, too."

His hands tightened around her waist. "Would you mind repeating that?"

She laughed out loud. "I love you, Judd Harwood. Love you, love you, love you...is that enough repetitions?"

He said in a dazed voice, "I don't think I can have too many. You're sure, Lise?"

"As sure as I'm standing here wrapped in a very damp towel. Judd, dear Judd, I love you with all my heart."

He pulled her closer. Then he lowered his head, kissing her as though there was no tomorrow. As though, Lise thought exultantly, he held paradise in his arms. She looped her hands around his neck, feeling the heat of his skin burn into hers, glorying in the thrust of his tongue and fierce pressure of his mouth.

Judd raised his head long enough to mutter, "The towel's slipping."

"So it is," she said demurely.

Laughter sparked his eyes. "What are you going to do about it?"

"How about nothing? Letting nature take its course?"

"Lise," he said with sudden urgency, "you will marry me?"

"Yes. Oh, yes, Judd. It would make me happier than I've ever imagined I could be."

"Thank God," Judd said. "It's more than I deserve. I was so insistent that I never wanted to commit myself to anyone other than Emmy that I refused to see what was right under my nose. You. Stubborn. Hot-tempered. Fiery and passionate."

She chuckled. "Not half as stubborn as you."

"Stop interrupting," he said, kissing the tip of her nose. "I not only shut you out. I was also hell-bent on denying

I'd fallen in love with you. I'm sorry, sweetheart. Truly sorry."

His lips were now wandering down her cheek to her throat. She said shakily, "You're forgiven."

"Did I also say you're astonishingly generous?"

He'd found the curve of her breast; the towel was now around her hips and her whole body was one ache of desire. "I don't think you mentioned that," she whispered, dropping kisses on his thick black hair. "I'm so happy, I'm almost scared to believe this is all true. I'm not going to wake up, am I?"

He straightened, drawing her closer. "The only place you're going to wake up is in my arms. In my bed. Lise, I swear I'll always be here for you. That I love you with all the strength in my body and the power of my soul."

Touched to the core, Lise said softly, "That's the most beautiful thing anyone's ever said to me. Oh, Judd, I do love you."

He said, "Let's go to bed. Now. Because sometimes words just aren't enough." Then his smile broke through. "Besides, I want to see you wearing nothing but an emerald and two sapphires."

"You think I'll look okay like that?"

"I know you will," he said, and set out to convince he was right.

Not that she took much convincing.

EPILOGUE

THE next morning the alarm clock woke Lise with a jump. As she reached over to flip the switch, she realized first that she was stark naked and secondly that she was in Judd's bed. He said lazily, "Good morning...how did you sleep?"

"Very little," she said, blushing. "Thanks to you."

"I aim to please."

"Oh," she said, "you do, you do."

"I'd better get up. Just in case Emmy comes looking for me. Good thing we set the alarm." He slid a hand down her hip. "Still love me?"

"More than ever. If that's possible."

"Perhaps," he said, his slate-gray eyes very serious, "love just keeps on growing."

"We could hang around each other and find out."

"What a good idea." His fingers circled her belly suggestively. "There's nothing I'd like better than to spend the morning in bed with you. But duty, in the form of my daughter, calls." He hesitated. "She'll be our daughter, Lise. Because Angeline's heading back to Europe—all her contacts are there. How do you feel about being Emmy's stepmother?"

"I love her already," Lise said simply.

"Let's tell her at breakfast that you're planning on staying. Forever."

Because she felt almost languid with happiness, it was half an hour before Lise slipped into her seat at the breakfast table. Judd and Emmy were already there. Emmy said cheerfully, "Did you have a nice time last night?"

185

For a moment all Lise could think of was the hours she'd spent in Judd's arms making love. Then she remembered the gala and her long green dress. "Oh, yes, it was lovely," she gabbled. "How about you? Was the popcorn good?"

"Fabulous." A faint shadow of anxiety crossed Emmy's face. "My friend Charlene phoned this morning. She forgot to tell me yesterday that our school concert's in three weeks. You'll still be here, won't you, Lise? Will you come to it?"

Lise smiled at her. "Yes, I'll be here. And I'd love to come to the concert." She glanced over at Judd, feeling absurdly shy. "Actually, we have something to tell you, Emmy."

Judd reached across the table and took Lise's hand in his. "How would you feel about Lise and me getting married, Emmy? That way Lise would always be here."

Emmy's big blue eyes went from her father to Lise. "Married?" she squeaked. "For real?"

"Definitely for real," Judd said. "For real and forever."

"That's a great idea! You wait til I tell Charlene."

Lise had tears in her eyes. "I'm so glad you're happy."

Emmy shoved back her chair and ran around the table to hug Lise; her long black hair smelled sweetly of shampoo. "Course I am. You're fun and real and brave."

It was an interesting endorsement, thought Lise, smiling through her tears. "I also make very good chocolate maple fudge—did I ever tell you that?"

"Yummy." Then Emmy pulled back, gazing speculatively from Lise to her father. "I've got a question. D'you think sometime you could make me a baby brother or sister? Charlene has one of each and they're kind of cute."

"I'm sure we could manage that," Judd said with a straight face. "Would you mind if it was fairly soon?"

"Oh, no." Emmy gave Lise a kiss flavored with pancake syrup, and hugged her father. "I've got such a lot to tell all the kids at school," she crowed. "Oh, I'm so excited. Can I be a bridesmaid?"

"Sure," said Judd. "We'd better pick a date. How about two weeks from Saturday, Lise?"

"Fine," Lise said breathlessly.

"Maybe some of the fire trucks could come," Emmy said, her head to one side. "Like in a parade."

"A quiet wedding," Judd said firmly.

"I bet if I have a brother or sister it'll have red hair," Emmy added artlessly.

And indeed when Matthew Judd Harwood was born seven and a half months later, he had unwinking slate-blue eyes and a thick fuzz of bright red hair.

Harlequin Presents®
and
Harlequin Romance®
have come together to celebrate a year of royalty

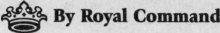 **By Royal Command**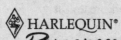

HARLEQUIN®
Romance®

EMOTIONALLY EXHILARATING!

Coming in June 2002

His Majesty's Marriage, #3703
Two original short stories by **Lucy Gordan** and **Rebecca Winters**

On-sale July 2002

The Prince's Proposal, #3709
by **Sophie Weston**

HARLEQUIN®
Presents

Seduction and Passion Guaranteed!

Coming in August 2002

Society Weddings, #2268
Two original short stories by **Sharon Kendrick** and **Kate Walker**

On-sale September 2002

The Prince's Pleasure, #2274
by **Robyn Donald**

**Escape into the exclusive world of royalty with
our royally themed books**

Available wherever Harlequin books are sold.

HARLEQUIN®
Makes any time special ®

The world's bestselling romance series.

Seduction and Passion Guaranteed!

*She's his in the bedroom,
but he can't buy her love...*

**The ultimate fantasy becomes reality in
Harlequin Presents®**

Live the dream with more *Mistress to a Millionaire*
titles by your favorite authors

Coming in July
THE UNEXPECTED MISTRESS
by Sara Wood, #2263

**Pick up a Harlequin Presents novel and you will
enter a world of spine-tingling passion and
provocative, tantalizing romance!**

Available wherever Harlequin books are sold.

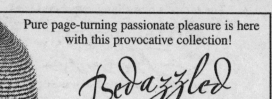

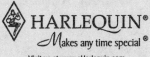